THE
FIREBUG
MYSTERY

THE FIREBUG MYSTERY

Mary Blount Christian

Cover and Frontispiece by Allen Davis

ALBERT WHITMAN & COMPANY, CHICAGO

Library of Congress Cataloging in Publication Data

Christian, Mary Blount.
    The firebug mystery.

    Summary: When half-finished buildings keep
burning around town, Brock and Gaby are shocked
to find that their own fathers are prime suspects.
    [1. Mystery and detective stories. 2. Arson—
Fiction] I. Davis, Allen, ill. II. Title.
PZ7.C4528Fh   [Fic]   81-11493
ISBN 0-8075-2444-1   AACR2

Text © 1982 by Mary Blount Christian
Illustrations © 1982 by Allen Davis
Published simultaneously in Canada by General Publishing, Limited, Toronto

Remembering Hazel and Frank Blount

1

The sirens screamed past the house in rapid succession. The pumper, the hook and ladder, then the chief's car—still the noise didn't stop.

Brock Everett reached toward his bedside table and pulled his alarm clock closer. He grabbed for his glasses and pushed them over his freckled nose. Squinting at the luminous dial, he read, 2:15 A.M.

The wailing sounds seemed to converge from every direction. More fire trucks and probably some police cars—it must be a big one.

Brock sniffed the air. No smoke here, he assured himself. He replaced his glasses on the table, then settled back again. He closed his eyes, pulled the covers tightly to his chin, and fell into a light sleep.

But the sudden raucous ring of the telephone brought him to attention again. Brock sat up, aware of a thin line of light under his closed door. He could hear his father's voice, muffled and guarded, then the phone being slammed into its cradle.

Footsteps quickened past his door and back to his parents' bedroom. Wire hangers scraped the rod as clothes were hastily snatched.

Brock rubbed his forehead groggily. He flipped back the covers, felt for his slippers, and groped his way through the dark to the door.

His dad came from the bedroom grim-faced, the corner of his mouth twitching nervously the way it did when he was under pressure. He had on his hard hat, the one he wore on the job.

"Dad?" Brock said, still rubbing his eyes sleepily.

"Another fire," Sam Everett mumbled. "One of our construction sites." He pushed through the back door and into the dark.

In a moment Brock heard the truck motor turning over, then all was silent again. He went into his room and turned on his radio to the all-night news station. They were already giving a short bulletin on the fire.

It was in the apartments under construction at West and Brady, the announcer said. A four-alarmer out of control and burning rapidly.

Quickly Brock dressed and slipped quietly past his mother's door. He left the house, carefully closing the screen door behind him.

He grabbed his bike and pedaled swiftly toward West and Brady. As he approached, Brock found that traffic was already snarled.

Television crews and a scattering of radio and newspaper reporters had double-parked their cars along the narrow streets, creating a bottleneck. The project was in a residential area, and people poured from their houses, attracted by the noise and light. Some stood watching curiously. Others watered their roofs with garden hoses.

A couple of fire fighters ran up and down the streets yelling for people to turn off their hoses so there would be enough water pressure to fight the fire.

The police were holding cars back, but Brock easily glided his bike past the makeshift barricades and joined the crowd of pedestrians that were as close as the police would allow them.

The entire area was aglow from the fire. Cinders and sparks were jettisoned in every direction.

Brock stared at the skeleton of what had been a half-completed apartment building, now totally engulfed in angry orange flames.

9

A wall gave way, and there were shouts of warning as it fell into the center of the blaze. Fireballs shot into the air, and the thick black smoke rolled like tumbleweeds across the sky.

Brock saw his father inside the barricade, nodding and motioning, conferring with a fire fighter in a white helmet. He was probably the captain.

Mr. Gifford was there, too. Garwood Gifford was the owner of the building and the contractor for the job. He was Mr. Everett's boss and the father of Brock's best friend, Gaby. Mr. Gifford stood still, his hands in his pockets, staring at the fire. Gaby stood by him, her hand resting comfortingly on his arm.

Brock thought what a rotten break this was for Mr. Gifford, especially on top of all his other problems.

Another of his projects had burned about a month before. Mr. Gifford looked like he was losing weight, and lately he was always popping some kind of stomach-calming pill.

Gaby said he was snappish and anxious all the time. He was worried about going bankrupt. He wanted to sell off a couple of his projects and concentrate on just one or two. But Gaby said he couldn't get any buyers.

10

For this project—the one that was now burning—some materials had been delivered late, delaying the job. Other things, like appliances, had come early and gotten in the way.

Brock's father said that in the building business you could always count on Murphy's law—what can go wrong will. The law seemed to be working overtime for Mr. Gifford these days.

The mobile television news crews were filming the fire, the crowd, and everything else remotely interesting. One man shoved a mike at Mr. Gifford and at Brock's father, but Brock couldn't hear what they were saying.

When the fire had died down some, Brock let his eyes roam over the crowd, which seemed to be in a lighter mood now that there was no more danger of the fire spreading. It was odd how some people reacted to fires—not with horror, but with a kind of fascination, as if they would gladly throw a match into a haystack, just to see it consumed by licking, lashing flames.

"Hi, Brock." A nasal, whining voice spoke to him.

Without turning, Brock knew the voice belonged to Humphrey Hamm, better known around school as "the Hump." Brock frowned uneasily. He didn't like the Hump. He didn't seem to have any real friends. He was always hanging just on the outskirts of the chattering groups at school—never participating, always hovering, listening. Ever since he was a little kid he had been a whiner and a tattletale. He didn't exactly have the traits you look for when picking a friend.

Brock shrugged a casual hello, hoping that no one would think the Hump was with him.

"Wasn't it beautiful?" Humphrey asked. His eyes searched Brock's face, as if looking for agreement. "I think I got some terrific pictures."

"Pictures!" Brock said, wrinkling his nose in disgust. "You're sick! Why'd you want pictures of something like this?"

Brock couldn't remember seeing Humphrey without his heavy camera with its special lens hanging around his neck. And there was always that uncomfortable fear that at any moment the Hump would set off his flash, freeze some very private moment onto film, and then pass it around to strangers and friends. Like the time he had taken a picture of Brock trying to get lettuce from between his teeth! The Hump was a real pain.

Humphrey moved on, still taking pictures as the

fire fighters began flattening and rolling up their excess hose.

Only one pumper and hook and ladder stayed behind to watch over the still-hot embers for the rest of the night.

The crowd dispersed. Mr. Everett spotted his son and frowned his disapproval that Brock was there. Then, apparently deciding not to scold him, he motioned for Brock to come with him.

"Put your bike in back of the truck," Mr. Everett said. "I'll take you home. There's nothing more to be done here tonight."

Brock noticed fatigue circles under his father's eyes and worry lines etched across his face. "What rotten luck," Brock said as he slid into the cool cab of the truck.

"Luck," his father repeated absently. "Maybe. Maybe that's what it was."

Brock frowned at him in the dark. "What do you mean? Do you think there's more to it?" he asked anxiously.

Mr. Everett pushed the truck into gear. "The captain said the fire looked as if it had started from a barrel of roofing tar. Maybe because a cigarette dropped into it."

"Wow!" Brock exclaimed. "That would have been so careless of somebody! Do you think one of your men was smoking?"

Mr. Everett turned into their driveway and shut off the motor. He helped Brock lift the bike to the ground.

"You know how I feel about smoking on a construction job!" Mr. Everett reminded him. "The men can punch out and go to one of the designated areas if they want to smoke. But I have NEVER allowed my men to smoke around the materials. Never!" His jaw was squared in grim determination.

"Yeah, Dad. I know. I know," Brock soothed. "But maybe someone was sneaking a cigarette."

The two stepped into the house, pausing in the kitchen to pour themselves generous glasses of milk.

"I guess someone could have sneaked a smoke," Mr. Everett said. "But another thing bothers me, Son. I know there were no barrels of tar left out. I inspected the area myself, just like I always do, before I left. All the barrels were locked inside the supply shed, next to the security guard's building."

"Are you sure?" Brock asked. Until the first fire a month ago, his father's reputation for being organized and thorough had been flawless.

14

"I'm positive. I'm absolutely positive, without any doubt. There were no barrels of anything flammable left in that area. After what happened last month I've been checking the construction sites every night myself. I wouldn't leave anything that important to someone else."

"Then what you're saying, Dad, is that the fire may not have been just an accident!"

Brock's father sighed, rising to run water into his empty glass and place it in the sink. "Of course, we'll know a lot more after we have a chance to look around in the daylight. But at this moment, it seems to me the fire was deliberately set. And maybe the one last month was, too."

Brock slowly set his glass down, not taking his eyes from his father's anxious face. "You mean arson?" The word was so frightening it nearly stuck in his throat. "A firebug? But who'd want to burn down half-finished buildings?"

Mr. Everett shrugged wearily. "The possibilities are endless, I suppose. Someone with a grudge, maybe, like someone I fired. Maybe a person who just hates someone or something connected with the job. Who knows, maybe even—" Mr. Everett seemed to shake off an ugly thought.

15

"Even what, Dad?" Brock insisted.

"Maybe even someone who wants the insurance money," Mr. Everett replied. "A project like this is insured for a great deal of money."

"Dad!" Brock was stunned by the thought.

The corner of Mr. Everett's mouth twitched. "I know. I don't believe it, either. There're rumors though—talk about Gifford's money problems. Arson investigators will be called in to consider that possibility. Of course, it's hard to accept. I've known Garwood Gifford for twenty years and have been working for him for eighteen. I'd sooner believe that *I* was careless than think Gifford's involved in some ugly insurance thing."

Brock stared, open-mouthed. There was another answer—there had to be!

2

The aroma of pancakes, warm and steaming, awakened Brock from his troubled sleep.

He looked forward to these unrushed Saturday breakfasts, even though his little sister did sometimes spoil things by acting her age, which was almost five.

"Put down the syrup, Marilla," Mrs. Everett scolded. "You mustn't drown your pancakes."

Brock grabbed the syrup bottle, which was as sticky on the outside as it was on the inside. Giving Marilla a disgruntled look, he asked, "Where's Dad?"

"Checking the ruins," Mrs. Everett replied.

"I didn't do it," Marilla protested.

Brock chuckled. "You probably ruined Pompeii, too," he teased, tugging gently at one of her red braids.

"Who's Pompy? What ruins?" Marilla asked.

17

"I have to prepare a brief for court this morning," Mrs. Everett reminded Brock. "I need you to sit with Marilla."

"What ruins?" Marilla asked, louder this time.

"Marilla needs a keeper, not a sitter," Brock said, laughing.

"I want somebody to LISTEN to me!" Marilla hollered.

"What's the matter?" Mrs. Everett asked her.

"What ruins?" Marilla persisted.

Mrs. Everett sighed. "There was a fire last night. I'm surprised you didn't hear the sirens."

"Yeah," Brock teased. "They sounded just like you, Marilla."

She made a face at him just as the door buzzer rang two longs and a short. Recognizing Gaby's familiar signal, Brock ran to let her in.

Gaby stood on the porch in her faded coveralls, her hair in one long braid behind her back. She looked more like a little girl than someone almost sixteen.

Brock grinned at her, feeling suddenly awkward, and blushed. This is ridiculous, he told himself, taking a deep breath. We grew up together. It's dumb to start getting serious.

Gaby shifted the bundle of cloth in her arms. "Hurry," she said. "I'm about to drop this. Did you remember the heavy-duty glue?"

Brock nodded. "It's in the garage. Want some pancakes? Mom kept a few warm for you."

"Sure," Gaby said. She put the cloth on the floor, nodded her greetings to Mrs. Everett and Marilla, and wrapped her slim frame into a kitchen chair. She immediately set to work on the pancakes. That was another thing Brock liked about Gaby. She wasn't a finicky eater.

"I'm really sorry about the fire, Gabrielle," Mrs. Everett said. "Is your father over there this morning?"

"Yes'm," Gaby answered, shoving a forkful of pancakes into her mouth. "It'll be a long morning. He wanted to stay with the investigators."

Mrs. Everett gathered the remaining dishes into the dishwasher and pushed the button. The machine wheezed, made scraunching noises, and finally gave out a whistling sound as the water poured in.

"I'll be so glad when I'm rid of that thing!" she grumbled.

"How are your plans for the new house coming?" Gaby asked.

"Beautifully—I hope. The architect'll bring them

over tonight. We should save a lot with Sam doing his own contracting."

Mrs. Everett reminded Brock to watch Marilla, then went into the den and closed the door behind her.

"What are we doing today?" Marilla asked, following Brock and Gaby out the back door.

"We're going to build the terrain for Brock's model railroad," Gaby answered.

Marilla looked puzzled. "How're you going to get his train into one of those little bottles?"

Gaby smiled. "You're thinking of a terrarium, honey. I mean we're going to make mountains and valleys and rivers on his trainboard."

Gaby poured glue into a large metal tub. "Now add an equal amount of water," she told Brock. She stirred with a wood spoon while he poured. When the solution looked thin enough, they dipped the cloth in.

"Do you think the fire was deliberate?" Brock asked as he squeezed some of the glue out.

"Of course not," Gaby said. "It was just an unfortunate mistake. Carelessness, that's all. Be sure all the cloth is wet."

Brock could feel his face burning as they lifted the glue-soaked cloth to the plywood board he'd mounted on legs. "Meaning my dad is responsible, I suppose?" he answered through clenched teeth.

"I didn't say that, Brock Everett," Gaby said. "The fire is over with, anyway. All that's left are the cleanup and the starting over."

Brock worked, tight-lipped. He was trying to resist the temptation to remind Gaby about the insurance money and her father's financial problems. After all, she knew her dad was having troubles, and she was probably worried herself.

They pushed and kneaded the cloth silently. The heavy material began to look like a mountain range.

"When it's dry next week we'll add the trees and —oh, no!" Gaby yelped. "Marilla!"

Brock whirled to see his little sister covered with glue and climbing from the bag of mulch in the corner. Shredded dried leaves clung to her.

He was almost grateful for the distraction. At least it kept him and Gaby from saying hurtful things to each other.

"Ugh!" Brock moaned, a laugh playing across his face. "It'd be easier to get another sister than to clean this one up!"

"Don't throw me away!" Marilla screamed.

"Oh, honey," Brock soothed. "I'm only kidding."

He hosed off most of the glue, then Gaby bathed Marilla while he cleaned up the mess in the garage.

In a short time Marilla, squeaky clean, bounced cheerily into the yard. She leaped onto her swing singing, "Rub-a-dub-dub, three men in a tub."

Brock grabbed Gaby's hand and pulled her to the back-porch steps. "I have a feeling this fire thing could get messy, Gaby. And I don't want it to come between us—not us."

She opened her mouth to reply. But before she had a chance, they were interrupted by the nasal greeting of Humphrey Hamm. He stood by the steps, a folder of photographs tucked under his arm, the silver ankh he wore on a chain catching the sunlight. The ankh was like those symbols of life the Egyptians wore, a T-shaped cross with a loop at the top.

"Well, if it isn't the siren-chaser," Brock said. For once he was actually glad to see the Hump. He didn't want to say any more that might hurt Gaby. And he didn't want to hear her ideas about the fire, either.

"Sit down, Hump. Are those pictures of the fire already? Let me see what you've got."

3

Brock thumbed through Humphrey's photographs. He was impressed. They were good, he had to admit, if pictures of something bad could be called good.

He went through the pictures again, this time slowly, carefully. Maybe he could find a clue to the fires. But what was he supposed to be looking for?

He handed the photos to Gaby, and she studied them, too. If she saw anything suspicious, she didn't say anything.

"You said you developed these last night. You got your own darkroom?" Brock asked Humphrey. "I didn't know you could get pictures this fast."

"It doesn't even take an hour, if you don't mind them turning brown eventually. I souped the negatives for the right time, then rushed these glossies through. I'll take my time making permanent ones, as soon as I decide which ones I want to keep.

23

"The whole basement is mine," Humphrey went on. "I've got developing tanks, an enlarger, everything. You and Gabrielle should come and see." He grinned. "I think these are the best fire pictures I ever took," he added, obvious pride in his voice.

"The best?" Brock said. "You mean you do this all the time?"

"Oh sure!" Humphrey bragged. "I have an emergency C.B. radio. I follow all the fires. You want to see some of my other shots?"

Brock curled his lip in distaste. "No, thanks. Hump, you must be a barrel of laughs at a wreck."

Humphrey nodded eagerly, shoving a picture toward Gaby. "Would you like your picture? I took it last night. You can have it, if you want it."

"Ah, thanks, Humphrey," Gaby said. "But I wouldn't want to break up the set."

There was a soft expression, a tenderness mirrored on Humphrey's face as he spoke to Gaby. Brock felt a tinge of jealousy flicker in himself. Did Humphrey have a crush on Gaby? he wondered.

The Hump fingered his silver ankh, twisting it on its chain nervously. "No, really. I want you to have it." He shoved the photo into Gaby's hands and left almost as suddenly as he'd appeared.

24

"Who was that masked man?" Brock asked in his best western accent. Then his grin faded as his eyes fell on the picture Humphrey had left. He stared somberly at it.

"Don't you think that's weird?" he asked Gaby.

"How do you expect me to look at three in the morning?" she asked indignantly.

"No, silly. I mean this thing Humphrey has about fires. Listening for them on the emergency radio all the time and going to take pictures—don't you think that's weird?"

"Yeah, I guess," Gaby replied. "But don't forget, some people think we're weird with our model railroading."

Brock brushed aside her comment. Model railroading was a longtime accepted hobby. There were railroading clubs and magazines and even whole hobby shops devoted to trains.

"Who ever heard of a store or magazine for fire buffs?" Brock asked.

A wicked smile played across Gaby's face. "Haven't you ever seen stores advertising fire sales before?"

They were still laughing when Brock's father rounded the corner of the house, his shoulders slumped slightly, his hands stuffed into his pants pockets.

Brock detected the twitch at the corner of his dad's mouth. "Dad?" he said. "Everything okay?"

Mr. Everett heaved a heavy sigh and sank to the step. "Gifford says it's going to be months before that job can reopen, if it ever does," he told them. "Meanwhile, there will be a lot of my men without work."

"Why won't the building start over right away?" Gaby asked. "I know Daddy had the project insured."

Mr. Everett nodded. "I don't really understand the delay. Surely your father must have had the apartment building insured for its replacement value instead of its purchase value. But that isn't anything I'd know about."

"Its replacement value?" Brock asked. "Of course! He would get a lot more insurance money back than he put in. Otherwise, with the prices going up all the time, he couldn't build half the apartment again."

"Right," Brock's father said. "If he wasn't getting more insurance money, he'd have to refinance the whole project. And that would mean higher interest rates, too."

Brock scowled, thinking. Unless Mr. Gifford had replacement insurance, it might be next to impossible to get money to rebuild. Especially with those two fires on the records.

"It's good you have those other projects spread out over the city," Brock said.

"I can absorb some of my men into those other projects—if I'm still working for Garwood, that is."

Brock felt a shock wave through his body. "Why wouldn't you be?"

"This is the second fire in a month. If they don't find the real cause, it'll look as if it was my fault. That isn't a very good job recommendation, is it?"

"You've worked for my father a long time, Mr. Everett," Gaby said. "He wouldn't let a lapse into carelessness ruin your record!"

Brock stiffened. He felt words explode from his mouth. "That's really generous of your father—particularly since it maybe was something a bit more serious than carelessness, Gaby!"

Gaby stood up. "What are you getting at, Brock?"

The angry words tumbled from him, brittle and biting. "I'm talking about insurance, Gabrielle. Money? Or don't you think that's possible?"

Gaby's eyes clouded, like the sky before a thunderstorm. Instead of replying, she turned on her heels and stalked away.

Brock was furious with himself for acting so stupid. Why had he jumped at Gaby like that? "Gaby?" he called after her.

"Go after her, Son. Don't let this thing make a mess of your friendship."

Brock's shoulders sagged in sudden, weary defeat. "Later—maybe. We both need some cool-off time, I think."

Maybe it was possible that one lousy barrel of tar had been overlooked. After all, his dad had jobs all over town to watch. Maybe he had been in a hurry to get to another job site. Maybe—

Hold it, Brock told himself. Whose side was he on, anyway? There were plenty of possibilities besides carelessness or greed. His dad wasn't slipshod on the job. And Mr. Gifford wasn't a crook.

A good detective always keeps an open mind. He doesn't abandon other possibilities.

Brock idly fingered the photo that Gaby had left behind.

4

After dinner Brock felt torn between seeing the architect's house plans and straightening things out with Gaby. He decided he had time for both.

He hovered over the kitchen table with his parents as Mark Markum explained the squiggles and scratches on the blueprints spread before them.

Marilla crept next to Brock. "Where's the house?" she asked. "I don't see a house."

"We've fooled around with these plans too long," Mr. Everett said. "We've got to get started. If we delay any longer, the house could cost us twice as much as we planned. Or maybe we'll wind up with only half the house we want. As it is, we'll have to cut a lot of extras."

29

"Not my beautiful fireplace!" Mrs. Everett moaned. "And my walk-in pantry?"

Markum heaved a sympathetic sigh. "I love drawing fireplaces and pantries, but they're generally scrubbed in the end."

The small voice at table-height wailed louder. "Where's the house?"

"It's a picture," Brock explained. "Pretend you're Superman with X-ray eyes looking down through the roof."

"Wonderwoman," she corrected indignantly. "But where's the smoke that comes out of the chimley?"

"That's *chimney*," Markum explained with a laugh. "Study these blueprints at your leisure, folks. And let me hear what you decide by next week, okay?"

Marilla settled on the floor to draw her own version of a house, complete with chimley. Brock left his parents to hammer out the details of the house and hurried to Gaby's.

He couldn't get something out of his mind. If costs were rising that fast, wouldn't inflation be affecting the apartment projects, too? Like his family, could Mr. Gifford be finding it difficult to pay for materials because their cost had risen so much since he'd first made his plans? Was he so squeezed by rising prices that he felt he had to get out of the projects—any way he could?

Brock paused briefly to get up his nerve, then rang Gaby's doorbell.

Gaby's expression was one of surprise turned into relief.

"Gaby—" Brock began.

"Forget it," she told him.

That was another thing Brock liked about Gaby. She might be as quick to anger as he. But she was also as quick to get over an argument.

A red Corvette pulled up in front of the Gifford house. The wheels made a swooshing noise as the woman hit the curb before coming to a stop.

Brock snickered. "Lousy driver," he commented.

A whiff of strong perfume invaded his nostrils as the woman clicked past them and up the steps to the Gifford house. She didn't acknowledge their presence. Brock raised a questioning eyebrow.

To his pleasant surprise Gaby grabbed his hand and pulled him along with her. "That's Allison," she said. "She and Dad are barbequing on the patio tonight. I'd like to disappear for a while."

Brock felt a twinge of disappointment that Gaby's joy at seeing him wasn't entirely due to his personal charm. "Not very friendly, is she?" he said.

Gaby giggled. "I prefer being ignored to being around those cheek-pinchers Dad dated when I was little!"

Brock squeezed her hand. "Want to go to a movie? There's a Japanese monster movie at the Main Street."

They got to the theater just in time, loaded up with popcorn, then hurried in before the lights dimmed.

"Looks like Noah's Ark, the way everyone's paired off," Gaby commented as they sat down.

Brock grinned, settling his arm lightly around her shoulder. "No need to look too conspicuous," he said with a wink, just in case she laughed at him. She didn't.

About midway through the movie, Brock saw a familiar figure move up the aisle toward the exit. "Good grief," he whispered. "Hump even carries his camera to the movies! Would you look at that?"

He was glad Humphrey was already gone when the lights came up. "I don't want to go home yet," Gaby told him. "Allison will still be there."

They ambled along Main Street, stopping with a few pedestrians gathered outside the window of the television store. One set was on, and the sound was connected to an outside speaker. Johnny Carson was exchanging quips with one of the Muppets.

They walked across the street to the pocket park, which glowed softly in the eerie bluish lights that dotted its walkways. The gazebo where the volunteer city band played concerts in the summer looked like a spectre in the shadows.

A few couples sat on the edge of the fountain, their shoes off and their feet dangling in the water, although the sign said that was strictly forbidden by city ordinance.

Brock and Gaby settled on one of the slat benches directly across from the fountain. Lacy shadows from the nearby pin oak danced across their faces. Only the constant splatter of the fountain broke the silence.

They sat holding hands, neither speaking for a while. Brock felt uncomfortable with the long, awkward quiet. Still, he was at a loss about what to say. He didn't dare bring up the fires, and it seemed dumb to talk about school, somehow. He cleared his throat. Gaby looked at him, as if she expected him to say something important.

"I'll sure be glad when the train board is finished."

"Me, too," she replied.

Dumb! he thought. Really dumb. He and Gaby never had any trouble talking before. Why now?

He sighed wearily and fell into silence again.

The air was suddenly shattered by the eerie wail of sirens. They both leaped to their feet, then stood frozen on the spot, staring at each other.

"Oh, Brock!" Gaby whispered. "No!"

Brock bit his lower lip uneasily. Houses burn. Stores burn. Even vacant lots burn. Fires were always starting. Odds were against this fire being in another one of Mr. Gifford's projects, he told himself.

Still the sirens wailed. It was another big one.

5

Brock ran, pulling Gaby with him. "Come on. We'll go back to that television shop. Maybe there'll be a news bulletin."

The two of them stood panting, waiting until the announcer cut in with the bulletin. The fire was in the Naughton apartment projects at Dawn and Lodge avenues.

Gaby allowed a huge sigh to escape her. "Oh, thank goodness! Those aren't Dad's."

Gently Brock touched her cheek. "I'm glad, too. Really glad." Brock was as relieved for Mr. Gifford as he was for his own father.

Hand in hand they strolled along the light-laced walks toward Gaby's house.

"It bothers me," Brock said. "I mean, even though it's not your dad's, another unfinished

35

apartment project is on fire. Don't you think that's kind of odd?"

"I don't know," Gaby said. "Houses burn all the time, and nobody ever says, 'hey—three houses this week.'"

"Well, at least this ought to take the pressure off our fathers, don't you think?" Brock asked hopefully.

"I—uh oh, wait here," Gaby said, tugging at Brock's arm. She nodded just ahead of them.

In front of Gaby's house, Allison leaned against her car. "The food was marvelous and the company dee-vine," she cooed to Mr. Gifford. "We *must* do this again."

She kissed him goodbye and roared off in her car, her headlights briefly brushing past Brock and Gaby.

The two of them stopped walking long enough for Mr. Gifford to return to the house. Then they moved onto the porch.

"The movie was marvelous and the company dee-vine," Gaby mimicked. "We *must* do this again." She brushed Brock's cheek with a kiss, then swooped into the house.

Brock stood frowning at the closed door. He wished Gaby wouldn't tease him like that. Why couldn't she be serious, just a little?

The next morning was Sunday. Mrs. Everett left before breakfast after learning that the client she was defending in an important case had been arrested trying to leave town. Mr. Everett left after breakfast to meet Mr. Gifford.

Brock got himself and Marilla ready for Sunday school. He apologized to the preacher that his parents weren't with them.

Later, as Brock was fixing lunch, Mrs. Everett stormed in, her briefcase hanging open and her papers flapping. She sank into a kitchen chair, grunting and muttering.

"Blast that man!" she hissed between clenched teeth. "I spent weeks preparing a perfectly good case for him. I even managed to get him out on bail while he waited for trial. And on the very eve of the trial he takes off for Mexico! They caught him at the airport. I could scream!" Her voice rose an octave.

Brock grinned at his mother. He flipped a sizzling patty onto a paper plate for her. "You just did."

She looked at him blankly. "Ummm, oh. I guess I did. Thanks for the burger. But why paper plates?"

"Marilla and I sort of pretend it's a picnic. That way we don't have anything to wash," he explained.

Brock's mother finished her burger, gave Brock a

friendly tweak on the ear, and left to change into her slacks. When she returned she said, "I'm afraid I have to break a bit of bad news to you. You know that train loft you wanted built in your new room? It'll have to be added later."

Brock shrugged off his disappointment. "That's okay. Really. My board in the garage'll be terrific. Gaby and I will get it fixed up pretty soon."

As he talked about Gaby, Brock felt his ears grow warm.

"We've dropped the idea of the landscaping, too," his mother added with a wistful sigh. "I'll root some cuttings from this yard so they'll be big enough to transplant by the time the house is finished. All those lovely plans. . ."

"I just don't understand how the cost got that out of hand," Brock said. "But at least you'll be adding your own personality to the new yard." He'd read that in a magazine somewhere and it seemed like a good thing to say.

"Ummm," Mrs. Everett replied. "All those weekends grubbing in the yard when I'd rather—oh, well."

"What about the chimley?" Marilla, who'd been attacking her burger with vigor, managed to ask.

Mrs. Everett sighed a martyr's sigh. "Gone, I'm afraid. Gone."

Brock saw his fantasy of himself and Gaby roasting marshmallows at the fireplace suddenly go poof. He rinsed off the skillet, then placed it in the dishwasher.

His civics class kept news clippings about the economy and got into hot debates on how to solve the inflation problem.

But Brock hadn't really cared about inflation until now, when it seemed to be affecting not only his family's building plans, but also his father's job.

Later Mr. Everett came home with the news that the apartment project had been delayed indefinitely. "It will take time to get the replacement values on the materials, the labor, etc. The whole job has to be refigured with the inflated prices," Mr. Everett told Brock.

"If the insurance company will pay at the new prices, then there's no problem, is there?" Brock asked.

Mr. Everett's mouth twitched slightly. "If rebuilding started now, there'd be no problem. But we can't wait. Six months or a year from now we could be in the same cost crunch. And Garwood is acting odd. Evasive. He doesn't want to talk about starting over. He just says, don't worry. Everything'll be all right. It's my hunch the jobs will never begin again. I think he'll just delay until everyone forgets about them.

"If I were superstitious," he went on, "I'd say the whole project was jinxed. Everything's gotten fouled up. Like those appliances, for instance. Even though we weren't ready to install them, they were delivered before the fire. Some foul-up in the order form, I guess. Of course, they were a total loss, too."

His father headed out to the garage. Soon Brock could hear him hammering, which was what he often did to beat away tension.

Brock finished up in the kitchen. If there was just some way he could prove his father was as good a construction foreman as he ever was, that someone had set the fires deliberately. But for what reason?

Money seemed the most likely motive. And if someone was trying to make money—or prevent himself from losing money—wouldn't that someone be Mr. Gifford?

Brock tried to push the ugly thought out of his mind, but somehow it seemed as hard as winning the old game he and Gaby used to play when they were kids. It was like not thinking about a purple bear once someone had planted the image in your mind.

40

6

All Sunday evening Brock mulled over his troubling thoughts.

His dad was convinced the fires weren't accidents. And the arson investigators must have been convinced too, or they wouldn't have been hanging around so much.

Everything seemed to point to Mr. Gifford. And now Brock's father said that it looked as if Mr. Gifford had decided against rebuilding, as if he just wanted to collect the insurance money, pay off his debts, and concentrate on his other projects.

Wasn't that what he had wanted to do in the first place—sell off some projects and stick with the ones that stood to make the most profit? Maybe when he didn't find a buyer, burning his buildings had seemed the only answer. No, Brock argued with himself. That wasn't like Mr. Gifford! He'd never been a quitter.

After school on Monday, Gaby loped over to join Brock under the pin oak on campus. Brock blushed guiltily at his thoughts about Mr. Gifford. Gaby would end their friendship on the spot if she knew how much he suspected her father.

"Is the board dry?" she asked him.

"Maybe," he replied. "I thought we'd check it out together. I'd like your opinion."

Gaby laughed. "My opinion? Dry is dry. You know dry when you see it. What's the matter with you, anyway?"

Brock scowled. "Nothing. Nothing's the matter. Why do you ask?"

Jay Yeoman strolled by and winked. "Aw, having a little squabble? Kiss and make up, now."

Brock growled in his direction. "Creep!" he muttered.

Gaby grinned. "Does it bother you? I mean, that Jay thinks we are, well, more than friends?"

"Good gosh, no!" Brock protested. "I mean, we are more than friends, aren't we? I want to be, that is." In his head the thought drummed at him: Prove her father guilty of arson and see if she wants to be more than your friend!

"I need a friend right now a whole lot," Gaby

42

said. "And I sure don't want to mess up our friendship by getting too serious. What if we got serious,
then broke up? I don't think we could ever be friends
again."

The thought of not being friends, not seeing
Gaby at all, hit Brock like a hammer between the
eyes. Maybe he shouldn't have said he wanted to be
more than a friend to Gaby. He felt cloddish and
stupid. All those books and movies about teenagers
made them seem so cool and smart. And it wasn't
like that at all with him.

The fire mystery was standing between him and
Gaby right now, and he was determined to find the
answer and get it out of the way.

"Just can't get serious about a freckle-faced
redhead who stumbles over his own feet all the time,
huh?" he said, trying to mask his concerns with
humor.

Gaby laughed, grabbing his hand. "You are such
a nut, Brock Everett. I can't think what I see in you,
to tell the truth." She gave him a sisterly peck on the
cheek as a pickup truck rumbled by.

"Way to go, Broccoli!" Jay Yeoman yelled.
"Yeee-ow!"

"Lousy creep," Brock mumbled. Still he grinned,

rather liking his new image of better-than-friend to the prettiest, smartest girl on campus. So what if Gaby didn't want to get serious just now. Jay didn't have to know it!

When they got to Brock's house, they checked the board and decided it was dry enough to work on.

"You sure you want this to be a winter scene?" Gaby asked.

"It seems easier. If the trees are bare we can use these little branches," he replied.

"It wouldn't be that much extra work to add leaves," Gaby said. "We can dip the branches into glue, then into the dried lichen and paint them."

"No," Brock decided. "Your board is a summer scene. If both train boards look alike we might get bored with them."

Gaby laughed. "Fat chance! Bored with model railroading? Never!"

They worked on the board until it was time for Brock to pick up Marilla from the day-care center. Gaby rode along with him, and Marilla perched on the handlebars of Brock's bike, chattering enthusiastically about her school project.

"We are making paperweights," she said. "We put our handprints into clay, then paint them. The teacher says our mommies and daddies will save them for posterior.''

While Gaby stifled a giggle, Brock patted Marilla on top of the head. "That's posterity, little one," he said, grinning.

"I'm going to give mine to Daddy so he won't be so unhappy," Marilla said.

Brock's grin faded. He glanced toward Gaby and saw that her expression had turned gloomy, too. The fire had become a wedge between them.

7

Later Brock stood in front of his full-length mirror, studying the reflection before him. He flexed his muscles, trying to detect even an encouraging ripple under his faded blue T-shirt. He sighed. Maybe he didn't have to look like a detective, just think like one.

"Brock?" his mother called from the kitchen. "What are you doing?"

"Er, nothing!" he called back. He went into the kitchen, where his mother was putting on some potatoes for supper. The family had taken turns getting the evening meal as long as he could remember. When it was Marilla's turn, she made a salad and they bought a pizza.

By the time Sam Everett got home, he had more

46

news about the house plans, which he said could wait until after they had eaten.

Brock figured the news couldn't be good or his father would have told them then and there. He was only waiting until after supper so their appetites wouldn't be spoiled. But knowing bad news was on its way spoiled Brock's appetite, anyway.

They ate in gloomy silence. Brock cleared the table and stacked the plates and glasses into the dishwasher. The machine wheezed and whistled the moment he pushed the starter button.

"We might just as well adjust ourselves to some more changes in the house plans right now," Mr. Everett began. "The cost of materials obviously is not going to go down. I have a crew ready to work and a loan officer standing by to make a final approval as soon as the plans are set.

"But there are always unavoidable delays, and costs are still going up by the month," Mr. Everett continued. "I have a choice of buying all the materials at first at the going price or buying them only as we use them and paying more for the last materials than for the first."

"It makes sense to buy it all now at the lower cost, doesn't it?" Brock asked.

"In some ways, yes. But then I'd have to hire a watchman to keep materials from being stolen. I figure the watchman or the higher-cost materials will come out to be the same extra cost," Mr. Everett explained.

"And once we're on paper with the loan company for certain features in the house, we have to stick to them," he added. "But with inflation, the loan just won't cover all the costs."

Mrs. Everett opened her mouth to say something, but before she could speak, Mr. Everett continued.

"We can't get as big a loan if we make the house smaller. We need the same square footage. That means we have to cut the cost by substituting and making do. Temporary things like carpet should be cheaper or omitted altogether. We can use pine instead of redwood, plaster board instead of decorator paneling—that sort of thing. Maybe we should even consider taking our old appliances with us instead of building in new ones."

"Sam!" Mrs. Everett wailed. "You surely don't mean that! You are shouting to be heard above that dishwasher now."

He shrugged. "It'd be cheaper to get it fixed, maybe. I'll find a repairman and get an estimate."

48

Mrs. Everett sank further into her chair. "We could save even more if we just stayed here. Or maybe we could live in a tent!"

"Gwen, don't be negative," Sam Everett told her. "I'm doing the best I can. I don't even know if I'll have a job to pay for this new house."

"They're going to fight!" Marilla wailed. "I hate it when they fight."

"Can we be excused?" Brock asked. He didn't much like it, either. Even though his family life class said that fighting was healthy, it made him nervous.

Mr. Everett dismissed them with a wave. Brock took Marilla for a bike ride and bought her some strawberry ice cream, the instant cure-all.

Later, Brock lay in bed, thinking. Saving money by using cheaper substitutes? Wouldn't someone make a profit if the insurance company repaid the cost of high quality materials when, in fact, cheap construction materials had been used?

There might have been substitutions after his father checked the materials. If the night watchmen were paid to look the other way, stuff could be hauled in and out practically all night long. But who was making the profit? A guard who just thought it would be a good way to make money? Mr. Gifford?

Brock scowled into the darkness. He was right back on that same old track, and it always stopped right at Mr. Gifford's feet. There was no way the father of such a wonderful girl could do such things, he told himself.

He pushed the cloudy thoughts from his mind. The phone was ringing. It was close to midnight. It was only then that Brock was aware of the sound of sirens. His skin crawled and his scalp felt tingly.

It couldn't be, he told himself. But the familiar sound of wire hangers scraping told him that his dad was going out.

There was another fire.

He turned on his radio. The fire was in one of his dad's buildings, the apartment project at Moran and Lomar. And from the news report, it sounded as if the whole thing was going.

He slipped on his clothes and crept out the back door to his bike. In moments he was pedaling toward the orange glow that lit the sky.

Mr. Gifford was already there. So was Gaby. She moved over to stand near Brock, slipping her arm through his so that he felt her trembling.

"Get that spaghetti unrolled!" the fire captain shouted. Brock could see why they called the hose spaghetti. Tangled in a heap on the ground, it looked just like spaghetti.

Sam Everett paced up and down, shouting and waving his arms. Only when he got close enough did Brock understand what he was shouting to the firemen, and his words sent chills through Brock like a shock wave.

"The night watchman!" Mr. Everett shouted. "Has anybody seen Mr. Long? Dear heaven, he must be in there!"

8

Brock could feel Gaby's grip tighten as the fire fighters rummaged up and down the blazing units, shouting to each other, clearing the way for themselves with their portable chemical sprayers.

He held his breath as one of them slipped through the fire. The blaze flared again behind the man, concealing him from view. It seemed like an eternity before he appeared again. This time he gingerly carried another man over his shoulder.

Word passed through the crowd of onlookers. The injured man was Mr. Long, the night watchman.

The fire fighter coughed and gagged, dropped to his knees under the load of the man, and then fell to the ground. Immediately the paramedics moved forward. They clamped oxygen masks onto both men. One shouted into a portable phone.

The fire fighter quickly revived. The medics placed the other man on a stretcher and into the ambulance. They sped away in a flash of lights and sirens.

Brock sighed with relief. If they were rushing, it meant that the watchman was still alive, at least.

Mr. Long had been unconscious when they found him. He had blood on the back of his head, probably the result of a falling beam, the captain told the television crew.

Brock spotted Humphrey squatting near the edge of the crowd, taking pictures as the work continued. "He's like a jackal following the lioness, just waiting for the leftovers," Brock told Gaby.

Humphrey strolled over to them. "Hi, fellow fire watchers," he said, grinning widely. "Did you see? They put the night watchman in that ambulance! Did you see?" Humphrey's shrill voice pierced the air.

"We know, Hump," Brock muttered. "You are such a lousy ghoul."

"This is the sixth apartment fire in town in the last six months," Humphrey said. "But this is the first injury in all that time."

"Sixth!" Brock echoed. "Are you sure?"

"Of course I'm sure," Humphrey said. "I have pictures of every one of them, too. All of them were only half-finished projects."

Brock pulled off his glasses and polished them on the edge of his T-shirt. "That seems too many for the law of averages, don't you think? I wondered about the fire in the Naughton apartments last week, too."

"Do you think maybe materials used in all the buildings have been flammable or faulty?" Gaby asked.

Humphrey snickered. "Flammable? Sure. Rub two sticks together, especially if one of 'em's a match. Then ftttttt!" He made a sizzling noise.

Brock glanced at Gaby. "That's a creepy thing to say, unless you know a lot more than you are letting on," he told Humphrey.

Humphrey cocked his head to one side in an obvious show of superiority. He fingered the silver chain around his neck. "You'll see," he repeated over his shoulder as he left them staring after him.

Brock's father came over to them. "You seem to be making as many fires as the pumpers. Put your bike in the back of the truck and let's go."

Brock noticed the corner of his dad's mouth twitching. He knew his father was agitated. He nodded to Gaby, then hurried to lift his bike into the truck. When he crawled into the cab with his father, he asked, "Is that night watchman going to be all right, Dad?"

"Dear heaven, I hope so," Mr. Everett said. "He's old—too old to be doing a night job, if you ask me. His age is against his recovery. I'm going to the hospital. He has no family."

"Let me go, too," Brock pleaded. "That way you won't have to take me home first."

"There's nothing you can do there, Brock. You don't even know him. Besides, you have school tomorrow."

"I won't be able to sleep anymore, anyway," Brock insisted. "I'm too uptight. I would like to be there—to be with you, Dad."

Mr. Everett gave his son a friendly slap on the shoulder. "Sometimes I forget that you're almost grown-up, Son. I—I'd like you to be there. Thanks."

In the hallway outside the emergency ward, Sam Everett called his wife. "Brock's here, too," he told her. There was a pause and Brock knew his mother must be questioning the need for him to stay up all night.

"It's okay, Gwen. He's a big comfort to me.

Maybe he can catnap here. He'll be all right, I promise."

Brock pulled a cup of black coffee from the coin machine in the waiting room for his dad. For himself he got a cola, then settled into a low vinyl chair. It made a whooshing sound as his weight forced it to his own contour.

They drank silently, each keeping an uneasy eye on the door from which a doctor would emerge any time now and tell them whether or not the old man would survive.

"Tom Long's worked in construction most of his life," Mr. Everett said. "He got too old to carpenter and took on jobs as night watchman. I guess he's good at it. He's the only one that Garwood hasn't fired in the last few months. He replaced all the others. Probably all of us would have come down hard on Garwood if he'd tried to get rid of Tom—he's well liked."

Brock was flushed with fear. Why had all the other watchmen been fired? Had Mr. Long's popularity cost him his life? Perhaps he wasn't up to coping with any vigorous vandals—or torchers.

The door to the emergency room swung open and a middle-aged doctor walked toward them. "You with the fire victim?" he asked. "You kin?"

"Friends," Mr. Everett said. "He has no relatives. Is he going to be all right?"

The doctor sighed slightly. "Well, he's taken in a lot of smoke. His heart beat's irregular and he has some lung damage, although we don't know how much just yet.

"That bump on the head was nasty. We're taking him to the operating room for stitches. We checked his scalp for splinters, but there are no wood fragments at all. Someone said a beam hit him?"

"We don't know for sure," Mr. Everett said. "That's probably what happened. May I see him?"

"He isn't conscious," the doctor said.

"I understand. I just want to see him for myself," Mr. Everett replied. He disappeared into the emergency room.

Brock waited outside, shifting uncomfortably from one foot to the other until his father emerged, walking beside the stretcher as they rolled Mr. Long toward the elevator.

The fragile old man looked pale, almost breakable. Tubes slowly fed glucose into his arm.

"He reminds me of Gramps," Brock said as he and his father climbed back into the truck later. He could tell that was what his dad was thinking, too.

"Why didn't Mr. Gifford come to the hospital tonight?" Brock wanted to know.

Sam Everett tensed his jaw. "I—I guess he's got his own problems right now. Maybe he just isn't thinking straight."

Brock didn't say any more. But he wasn't convinced that Garwood Gifford had a good excuse. What could be more important than seeing that Mr. Long was okay?

Something seemed all out of kilter, but Brock just couldn't put his finger on it. Why did Mr. Gifford fire all the old watchmen and hire new ones? Because the old watchmen would have noticed and reported the strange things that were going on? Why did all the facts keep pointing right back to Gaby's father, unless—

Brock's mind raced as he crawled back into bed. It was 5:30 A.M. There was only an hour before the alarm would ring for him to get ready for school.

He had just fallen into a kind of twilight sleep when it hit him. The doctor had said there were no wood splinters on the old man's head.

But wouldn't wood—especially new wood—leave splinters? For a beam to hit someone that hard something would have been left behind.

Maybe if he searched the site of the fire he could find the beam. But what if he couldn't?

He drifted into sleep with a thought that nagged and haunted him.

What if something else had hit the old man—something that didn't leave splinters. A pipe? A gun butt? Or a heavy camera, maybe?

Then what had happened to Mr. Long could no longer be considered an accident. It would have been attempted murder.

A camera? Now why did he think of that? Brock wondered sleepily.

Later he had a dream about a cat chasing a mouse. And the cat had a camera around its neck.

9

In the light of day the idea of old Humphrey hitting anyone with anything seemed silly, a figment of Brock's nightmares. Still, it wasn't impossible that the Hump had set the fires, was it?

"Any word on Mr. Long?" Brock asked his mother at breakfast.

"He's still unconscious," Mrs. Everett said, shaking her head. "It's just tragic."

She grabbed her briefcase with one hand and Marilla with the other. "See you this evening," she told Brock.

"I think I'll stop by the hospital on the way home," he told her. "Just to peek in, you know."

She bounded the back steps two at a time with Marilla in tow. "Good idea. See if he needs anything," she called back.

Brock swallowed the rest of his oatmeal. He decided to take his bike. That was the best way to get to the hospital and home again with time to spare, he figured.

Maybe he would have some time to check on Humphrey. His dream still haunted him. And he couldn't dismiss the fact that Hump was at every fire, that he knew so much about them and seemed to actually enjoy them.

Humphrey probably had had the opportunity to torch the projects. But why? There was no profit for him. Brock remembered the tender way Hump approached Gaby. Maybe he was trying to get her attention some way. Or did he just like fires?

Brock frowned. Was he just being too anxious to prove the fires weren't being set by the father of the girl he loved?

In the school yard he saw Gaby leaning against the oak, her eyes closed. She seemed unaware of the noisy chatter all around her.

"Tired?" he asked.

"Ummmm," she answered. "Really beat."

"Me too," he admitted. "We were at the hospital until around five this morning."

"How is the watchman?" she asked. "Dad was

still asleep when I left, so I didn't get a chance to ask him.''

Brock frowned. "How would he know, anyway? He wasn't at the hospital.''

Gaby's face paled. "He—he wasn't? But, I thought—are you sure?''

Brock didn't answer.

"He was horribly upset," Gaby said. "He dropped me off at home and didn't even wait to see that I got in okay. I thought he was going to hit a tree, he took off so fast.''

The warning bell rang, and Gaby gathered her books. The two of them strolled slowly toward the double doors where crowds of kids were shoving in.

"Gaby," Brock said in almost a whisper. "Is your father in some kind of trouble? Do you think—''

Gaby pulled her hand from his. "Brock Everett, don't you even think for a minute—" She pushed through the crowd and was out of earshot in an instant.

"Klutzmouth!" Brock scolded himself. "When are you going to learn to keep your big mouth shut?''

"Hi," the whining voice behind him said. "Are you talking to me?''

Brock whirled to see Humphrey just behind him,

his heavy camera hanging casually around his neck. He again remembered the cat in his dream. He decided not to blow his only lead that didn't include Gaby's father.

If Humphrey really was one of those firebugs he'd heard about, he had to find out. To clear Gaby's father. To make things more peaceful at home. And even to help Humphrey.

The Hump couldn't be setting fires for meanness. He might be weird, but he wasn't mean. He could get help. Maybe he could be cured.

Brock forced a smile across his freckled face. "Get some good pictures this time, Hump?" he asked.

Humphrey grinned broadly. "Oh, yeah! I brought 'em. Want to see?"

"How about at lunchtime?" Brock said.

Brock slipped inside his homeroom and dashed for his desk as the last bell rang. Before lunch he shared a social studies class with Humphrey. To Brock's dismay, he remembered it was oral report day.

Brock shifted uneasily as one student, then another, stood to talk. Finally it was Humphrey's turn. Brock stared. There was something different about the Hump this morning.

Maybe it was because he had had to leave his camera at his desk. He did look different without the camera hanging around his neck, Brock thought. Same silver chain around his neck. Same—

No! Brock realized. That medallion Humphrey wore on the chain was missing. Did he have it on at the fire last night? Brock tried to remember. He didn't think so.

At lunch break, Brock took his sack and drink to a shaded patch of grass outside. He didn't bother to look for Humphrey. There was no need. One thing about the Hump—you couldn't hide from him if you wanted to. And with Brock's invitation to encourage him, Humphrey would hunt the world over until they got together.

So Brock was not expecting to look up and see Gaby standing in front of him, clearing her throat. "I'm sorry I snapped," she said. "I—I'm just so scared, that's all."

"I'm sorry, too," he admitted. "I wouldn't hurt you for anything, Gaby. You know that."

She settled on the grass, and they'd just opened their lunch sacks when Humphrey squatted beside them.

"Here they are," Humphrey said. Looking at

64

Gaby, he added, "Brock asked to see my pictures!"

Brock crammed a dill pickle into his mouth, wiped his hands on the side of his jeans, and took the stack of glossies that Humphrey offered him.

Gaby leaned closer, shaking her head sadly. "It hurts to be reminded," she said.

Brock frowned. "Where are the fire trucks in these shots?" he asked.

"They hadn't got there yet," Humphrey said.

Brock raised a questioning eyebrow. "How did you beat them to the fire?" Unless you knew about it before they did, he added to himself.

Humphrey grinned. "I have an emergency radio. I know about fires as soon as anyone. And my house is closer to Moran and Lomar than the fire department is."

Brock shuffled through the pictures. There were several shots of the paramedics working on the fire fighter and on Mr. Long. Brock winced, remembering.

The Hump took good photos, he had to admit. It just seemed awful to have pictures of such pain. It was like an intrusion into privacy.

Brock spread the pictures on the grass, shifting them until he figured he had them in proper sequence. He studied them one at a time.

They looked almost like the photos of the other fire, really. Even the people were starting to look alike. He could swear he'd seen that guy in the business suit before, for instance.

He squinted at the man, trying to see his features more clearly. But the figure was out of focus. Brock shrugged. After all, he was in two sets of photos himself. Maybe the guy just liked to go to fires.

He pushed the pictures into a pile and shoved them toward Humphrey. "Thanks, Hump. You really are a good photographer."

Humphrey seemed to bask in the praise. Brock decided to pursue this further.

"You know what I'd really like?" he asked in the tone he took with Marilla when he wanted to talk her into something. "I'd like to see all of your pictures, Humphrey. I'd like to look at every single one of them, in the order you took them."

"Yeah?" Humphrey asked. "Great! you'll see how much I've improved since the first fire. I'm really getting good."

"Practice makes perfect, huh?" Brock asked. He wondered if that included arson.

Humphrey grinned his broadest grin ever. "You can see my darkroom and everything!"

"I'd like that," Brock said. "After school today? Is that all right?"

"All right?" Humphrey asked. "That's perfect!"

The bell rang. Brock winked at Gaby, who was staring at him with a look of complete bewilderment. Humphrey gathered his pictures and pushed himself to a standing position, grunting slightly.

Brock waited until Humphrey was walking away, then he sprang his big question.

"By the way, Hump, where's your medallion?"

Humphrey whirled toward Brock, fear etched across his face. His pudgy hand grasped at the empty chain.

"Lost it," Humphrey said, not looking at Brock. "Guess it fell off somewhere."

He turned and disappeared into the crowded hall.

10

Brock rubbed his chin thoughtfully as he watched Humphrey blend into the crowd.

"Are you nuts?" Gaby asked. "Why do you want to look at those horrible pictures? And why did you ask about his medallion? What's going on?"

Brock grinned. "There may be a clue in the pictures. There may be a clue in where his medallion is. And when I am sure what's going on, I'll let you know."

"I hope you weren't planning on my going with you," she said.

Brock laughed. "As a matter of fact, I was. Through thick and thin, better and worse and all that stuff. I'll meet you at my locker after school."

A look of mischief came over Gaby's face. "Well, I just don't know, Everett. You'll have to wait until this afternoon to see if I'm all that smitten with you!"

He was relieved when Gaby did meet him at the lockers after school. "So now I know you care," he said, tweaking her nose gratefully.

He threw his books into the locker, got the key to his bike lock, and grabbed Gaby's hand. "Come on. We've got a couple of stops before we see the Hump's pictures."

Gaby climbed on the banana seat behind him and wrapped her arms around his waist. Brock pushed off, happy to be taking action, at last. Maybe he'd soon have the answer to the fires.

They parked the bike next to a lamp post in front of the hospital. Brock ran the chain through the spokes and snapped it shut.

Inside they found the nurses' station. "Is there anything that Mr. Long needs?" Brock asked the nurse there. "Razor, clothes, stuff like that?"

"We won't take him out of hospital gowns until he gets much better," the nurse said. "We won't shave him, either. You can take a peek if you want, but make it a quick one."

Brock glanced at Gaby, who nodded to him that

she wanted to go, too. They stepped inside the room where Brock was immediately aware of machine noises. The oxygen machine made a rhythmic whooshing sound. Plastic tubes in Mr. Long's nose were connected to a machine that hummed and flashed. The glucose tube was still attached to his arm. He looked pale.

"What's that for?" Brock whispered, nodding toward the humming machine.

"It keeps his stomach clear of gas and other materials," the attendant replied. "Keeps him from getting sick."

Mr. Long tossed his head restlessly. "Gimme some more nails, Luke," he shouted in a slurred voice. "Nice job. Shame to tear down the old city hall, though."

Brock glanced anxiously at the nurse. She smiled reassuringly at him.

"Don't mind all that talk. He's a little out of it. It's because of his age and the anesthetic they used. It's hard on older people."

"That's quarter-inch board!" Mr. Long muttered. "I swear it was three-quarters here. And them nails—they ain't galvanized."

"Will it pass?" Brock asked, concerned.

"In three or four days, maybe a week," the nurse said. "Unless there are any complications, of course."

"Howdy, Mr. Gifford," the old man mumbled. "Them vandals are bad, they are. Watch out, Mr. Gifford! They done stole the good stuff and left junk."

Gaby looked away. "Poor man," she said.

"He's just replaying a few memory tapes, probably very old ones," the nurse said. "Garbling a few of them, too, no doubt. Anesthetic does that to some people. Time for you to go now."

Brock nodded his thanks. He and Gaby left, pedaling toward the burned-out apartment.

"What a terrible accident!" Gaby murmured. "That poor man."

"Do you still think it was an accident?" Brock asked. "What if Mr. Long saw someone setting a fire and that person saw him, too?"

"Brock!" Gaby said. "You surely don't still think—you can't mean he was hit on purpose!"

"I don't want to think so," Brock said. "But even you can't believe all of these fires are accidents anymore. Even if they look as if they start from combustion, somebody *has* to be doing this on purpose."

He stopped the bike at the edge of the apartment site. "I think the answers are right here. I know my dad isn't careless. And you know your dad isn't the kind of man that would—would—''

Gaby sighed. ''Go on and say it—the kind of man that would torch a building and hurt anybody. What kind would?''

Brock locked the bike. ''Come on,'' he said, tugging at her hand. ''I hope maybe the answer to that question is in there. And I don't want to say any more until I am sure.''

Gaby pulled back. ''But there is a watchman here,'' she said. ''I heard Daddy hire him.''

''You are the boss's daughter, aren't you?'' he chided.

She laughed. ''Now I see why I'm needed on this caper.''

''Bluff,'' he whispered. ''Act confident.''

The security guard trotted toward them. ''Hey, you kids! What are you doing here?''

Gaby nodded and smiled. ''Oh, Mr. Milroy! My father, Garwood Gifford, mentioned you'd be here. I'll remember to tell him that you are alert and ready.''

At the mention of Mr. Gifford's name, the man stopped, obviously flustered. He touched the bill of his cap, nodded, and went back to the guard shack.

"I hear a ball game on the radio in there," Brock said, grinning. "I'm sure he's more than glad to forget about us."

The ground was still sloshy from the gallons of water that had been poured on the fire. Gingerly Brock and Gaby stepped toward the middle of the burned-out shells.

"There," Brock said, pointing. "I think it was about there that they brought out Mr. Long. Don't you agree?"

"I believe so," Gaby agreed. "Why?"

"I'm not sure yet," Brock replied. "I just want to see for myself."

He stepped into what would have been the living room in the finished apartment. The smell of ash surrounded him. He looked up toward the charred skeleton of the rooms above. The sky was visible, but the beams seemed to be still in place.

Kitchen, bedroom, bath—it was hard now to know where they had once been. Appliances were strewn around—a dishwasher, refrigerator, range. But the place wasn't cluttered with fallen beams as Brock had expected.

If a beam had fallen on Mr. Long, where was it now? Wouldn't it still be in the same area? Brock looked up. The beams overhead were still in place. Charred, but in place.

Maybe something other than a beam had knocked out Mr. Long. Or maybe whatever hit him was burned or thrown outside by the fire fighters. There was no proof here that Mr. Long was hit on purpose.

The late afternoon sun filtered through the blackened wood. Its orange tint gave the framework an eerie firelike glow. Brock's eyes caught something shining in the smut-blackened puddle of water at his feet.

He stopped to pick it up. It was a bright silver medallion.

11

Brock turned the medallion over and over in his hand. It was Hump's all right. It had to be. He'd never seen another one quite like it. And Humphrey's had been missing from his chain this very same day.

But how did it get here in the fire debris? Unless—

"What did you find?" Gaby asked.

Brock opened his hand, revealing the medallion. Gaby stared at it. She turned frightened eyes toward Brock.

"Where did you find it?" she wanted to know.

"There," Brock said, pointing to the dark puddle of water.

"But how—?"

"I think there's only one answer," Brock said. "He wouldn't have been allowed in the area after the fire fighters arrived, so he must have been there

75

before the fire started. The Hump's a fire freak, a siren chaser. Maybe he got tired of chasing sirens.''

''What do you mean?''

''I mean, maybe he got tired of waiting for fires to happen on their own. Maybe he sets them so he can take his crazy pictures. Maybe he just likes to see them burn.''

''But Mr. Long—''

Brock shook his head disbelievingly. ''I know. I don't believe it, either. But maybe the Hump got scared. Maybe it was an accident. Maybe—'' His voice trailed off.

''I don't believe that,'' Gaby said. ''Humphrey may be different, strange. But he wouldn't—he couldn't!''

''You read about it sometimes,'' Brock reasoned. ''It's a sickness. People can't help themselves. But they can *be* helped. They can go to hospitals.''

Gaby's face mirrored her mounting horror. ''You mean, we should turn him in? But we couldn't! Insurance will make up most of the losses. And Mr. Long is going to be okay. We—''

''We don't know that Mr. Long will be okay. He may die!'' Brock yelled. ''And what about next time, or the next?''

Gaby hugged herself to Brock and buried her face in his shoulder. "Next time," she said. "Yes, there might be a next time."

"We're supposed to go over to Humphrey's, remember?" he said gently. "We'd better go. To tell you the truth, Gaby, I'm a little scared, too. I'm not sure I can go through this without you—without your help."

"Oh, Brock!" Gaby moaned. "I am not sure I can face him. I'm not sure I can look him in the face."

"We committed ourselves to finding the answer," he reminded her. "Let's go."

He followed Gaby toward the still-standing door frame, shoving the medallion into his pocket. Brock paused, looking back. Had he really found all the clues? Or had he stopped looking when he'd found the medallion?

He spotted the appliances again. Why had they been delivered so soon? Appliances weren't usually installed until the very end, were they?

They had been left crated and bunched in a corner. Some crates were badly charred. Some had burned away, and the appliances inside them were soot-black.

On impulse Brock went back and circled the charred

appliances a couple of times. What was bothering him about them? He ran his finger over the soot. Some of the enamel chipped off on his finger.

Knobs—that's what was bothering him. All the knobs, buttons, and handles were in place. It seemed to Brock that such things were usually bagged separately and put on after the appliances were installed.

Brock pulled at the handle on the dishwasher. The rubber seal had melted, fusing the lid shut. He managed to force it open and looked inside. He ran his fingers over a rust spot on the inside wall.

It was possible for the soot and fire damage to cover a lot of evidence on the outside of these appliances. But there was no mistaking the evidence he saw inside, where no one else had bothered to look.

He knelt to find the registration plate. He'd learned from his father a long time ago how to decode the numbers. With his handkerchief Brock gently wiped away the soot.

He could read the date of manufacture as clearly as if he'd been handed a store guarantee.

Brock checked another appliance, then another and another. They were all old machines in new crates. Had they been delivered this way? He wondered. Or had they been switched with new machines at some point? Was it possible that Mr. Long was aware of the switch?

What was it he'd said in the hospital—the nails weren't galvanized? And something about quarter-inch board that was supposed to be three-quarters of an inch? Maybe Mr. Long was talking about something that had happened long ago, but maybe the same thing was happening now. Maybe a lot of materials for the apartment projects had been switched—expensive materials for cheaper ones.

"Coming?" Gaby called. "I thought you were right behind me."

"Coming!" he called back, rising to brush off his pants. He trotted toward his bike, hoping the burden of his clues didn't show on his face.

How could he tell Gaby what he'd found? How could he tell her that those appliances were probably not the new ones the insurance company would pay for?

It looked as if someone had pulled a switch. Those machines were clearly ten years old.

And that brought him right back to the motive of arson for profit and to Mr. Gifford, his best friend's father, as the prime suspect.

12

As Brock slowly pedaled himself and Gaby toward Humphrey's house, he tried to work his way through the disturbing clues. The silver medallion put the Hump at the fire scene. But what did Humphrey have to do with switching appliances?

How did Humphrey's medallion fit together with the troublesome evidence that those appliances were not the new ones, the new ones that had been insured?

Brock thought more about the appliances. Were they the ones that had been originally delivered to the apartments? Wouldn't his father know if they were? Or had the appliances been switched at some time?

Of course his father's job was to supervise construction. He didn't worry about the cost of materials. He didn't sign or check in materials as they were delivered. And his dad wasn't at one place all the time—he drove from project to project all day. Anything could happen at one building while he was at another.

Could Mr. Long have known about the old appliances? Did he know about other materials that had been substituted as well, like the nails and plywood? Could he tell them what had happened once he regained consciousness? If he regained consciousness?

Mr. Long's injury troubled Brock, too. Had he been deliberately hit or had he fallen and struck his head on something?

The whole set-up looked more and more like some kind of insurance rip-off. Could Humphrey somehow have played into the hands of insurance crooks?

"What are you going to do about the medallion?" Gaby asked, breaking into his thoughts.

"I'm not sure," he answered honestly. He decided to play it by ear.

They rang the bell at Humphrey's house. A woman answered.

"You want to see Humphrey?" the woman asked almost with disbelief. It was as if he'd never had a visitor before.

"Come in!" she cooed at them. "I'll make some chocolate milk. Oh, it'll be so nice!"

"Er—no. Please, m'am," Gaby protested. "It's sort of close to supper."

"Nonsense!" she said. "Sweetie!" she yelled over her shoulder. "Company!" She padded off to the kitchen.

Brock and Gaby stared at the living room. It seemed dwarfed by over-stuffed furniture and by the bric-a-brac that cluttered every table and shelf. Dishes of bonbons and chocolate-covered peanuts were scattered around.

"You really did come!" Humphrey greeted them. "I—I thought maybe you'd changed your mind."

Brock mumbled, "I said we'd come, didn't I?"

"Yeah," Humphrey said. "But some of the others are always telling me they're coming, too. But they don't. I wait and wait—"

Brock felt a knot in his throat. "Yeah, well. Let's see those pictures of yours. I'd like to get a better look at the ones you showed me already. And I'd like to see the ones from the other fires, too. Maybe you have a clue in them and just don't know it."

Humphrey's face brightened. He led them through the kitchen and into the basement. The three of them made their way slowly down the wooden steps and into a room that was literally covered with glossy photos of fires. Several of the pictures were poster size.

"Good grief, I don't believe it!" Brock exclaimed. "I have never seen so many fire pictures in all my life."

Sweeping the air with his stocky arm, Humphrey said, "Start over here. See? They're labeled with the date and location."

Brock walked slowly around the room, pausing to examine a few of the pictures more closely.

"Just look at all that natural energy!" Humphrey said. "Yet people can never conquer it with man-made equipment. Did you know that most arson isn't even done by professionals? Most fires are set by kids."

Brock shuddered involuntarily. His eyes flicked from one glossy photo to the next. The pictures were breathtaking. For the first time he began to under-stand Humphrey's fascination with fires.

"Do you ever take pictures of fires when they are little?" Brock asked. "Just starting maybe?"

"Little fires aren't very interesting," Humphrey replied with a shrug. "Besides, they burn a long time inside before anyone ever notices them."

Brock studied Humphrey's face, looking for a clue to what he was thinking. "How do you know all that?"

"I've watched 'em."

"At close hand?" Brock asked.

Humphrey grinned broadly, making Brock feel uneasy. "Maybe," he replied.

Gaby tugged at Brock's arm. "I really need to get home," she said. Her eyes seemed pleading.

"I'll come back another time and look at them better," Brock promised. "I'd really like to study these pictures some more." It was obvious Humphrey wasn't going to mention he had left his medallion at the burned apartment project. Somehow Brock had to get the Hump to show his hand.

"Tomorrow?" Humphrey asked. "Come back tomorrow."

When they reached the top of the stairs, Mrs. Hamm was stacking cookies on a plate. "Oh, you're not going!" she exclaimed. "I was just about to serve you something."

Brock thanked her anyway. He decided it was time to spring the medallion on Humphrey, in front of his mother where it would be hard to make excuses.

"Oh, by the way, Humphrey. Is this yours?" He held the medallion out, watching for a reaction.

Humphrey grinned. His eyes never left Brock's. "Naw," he replied.

But his mother plucked the medallion from Brock's hand. "Of course it is, dearest! Look! It's got your initials scratched on the other side."

The phone rang and Mrs. Hamm left to answer it. Humphrey's face was still frozen into a grin. He said nothing, and he was still grinning when he let Brock and Gaby out of the house.

"I found it at the fire," Brock told Humphrey. "Inside where Mr. Long was."

Humphrey's expression didn't change.

"What I didn't find was anything that might have knocked out Mr. Long," Brock continued.

"Don't forget you're coming back to see more pictures," Humphrey said, at last, ignoring all Brock's remarks.

Brock and Gaby rode home in silence. Brock knew that now Gaby was probably convinced that Humphrey was setting the fires. Of course, she didn't know about the switched appliances. If only the whole thing weren't so confusing. Humphrey certainly acted guilty. And the medallion did point to him. But what about the appliances? How could the Hump be connected with them?

They pulled to a stop in front of Gaby's house. Brock could feel her tighten her hold.

"What's the matter?" he asked her.

"That car," she said. "I've seen it here before."

"A girl friend's?" he asked.

"No," Gaby replied. "It belongs to a man. I don't like him. He's been here a couple of times since the first fire. He makes Dad nervous. And he scares me a little."

"You want me to hang around?" Brock volunteered.

Gaby shook her head. "That's okay. They're probably in the den anyway, whispering as usual."

Brock gave Gaby an encouraging peck on the cheek, then pushed off on his bike. As he passed the car parked in front—the one that made Gaby feel so scared—he noticed it had a sticker on the back windshield. The sticker was from a car-rental agency.

He pedaled on, feeling his skin prickle as a siren rushed toward him from behind. The vehicle passed. It was an ambulance, not a fire truck.

Brock felt relieved, but only slightly. He knew he'd never really relax again until the firebug was off the streets. No matter who he was.

13

"I tell you, it's a nightmare!" Mrs. Everett muttered to Brock as he came into the kitchen.

He froze. "What?"

"They cleared the lot for our house this morning, and before I could leave court and get there on my lunch hour they'd cut down half the trees they weren't supposed to touch. Somehow they had the idea they were supposed to cut the ones that were marked. But those were the ones they were supposed to *save*.

"And they bulldozed that nice little hump in the front yard, too. Can you imagine? It was the only thing that made our lot look the least bit different from all the others, and they bulldozed it! Thought it'd be easier on the lawn mower!" Her voice had reached a shriek.

87

"Whew! I thought maybe there was something about the fire or about Mr. Long maybe."

His mother sighed. "Not that I know of. Mr. Long is the same. Your father is out at our lot now seeing what other damage was done in our absence."

Marilla stood on a stool at the sink, washing lettuce. She carefully dunked each leaf into the sinkful of water, then ceremoniously dried it with the mounds of paper toweling she'd gathered.

Water droplets clung to her lashes. "I hear Daddy!" she shouted.

In a moment Mr. Everett, his face glum and worry-lined, came in.

"I swear, Sam, if your face were hanging any lower I'd expect to see tire tracks on it," Gwen Everett said. She kissed him a light greeting.

"They poured the slab this afternoon," he said. "And it looks like rain. Figures."

"Any closer to solving the fires?" Brock asked.

"They rounded up a few vagrants," Mr. Everett said. "But the police are pretty sure that none of them set the fire, not even by accident."

"Vagrants!" Brock said. "You mean strangers?" He'd never considered that possibility before. The thought gave him some hope.

"Does Garwood still think these are all accidents?" Mrs. Everett asked.

"Yes—he's trying to call off the investigation. But fortunately, it's entirely in the hands of the arson people. And they'll keep poking around until they get an answer or something else demands their attention, I guess."

The thought of Mr. Gifford not particularly wanting the investigation to continue was disturbing to Brock. "Do they ever bring in guys from out of town?" he asked.

"Investigators, you mean? Not that I know of," Mr. Everett said. "Why?"

"No reason, I guess," Brock said with a shrug. He again wondered who the man with the rental car at Gaby's had been. If he wasn't an investigator, just who was he?

That very night the arson investigators came to talk with Mr. Everett. Brock let them in the living room and leaned against the door frame, hoping to hear what they said.

His father motioned for Brock to join them. "Come on, Son. This concerns us all and I certainly have nothing to keep secret. That is, if you gentlemen don't, either—"

The older man shrugged lightly, and Brock sat on the arm of his father's chair, leaning forward to catch every word.

"We have no doubt all the projects were torched," the older man said. "The first apartment project showed burn patterns indicating a flammable liquid was thrown all around. The second fire started when a barrel of roofing tar was ignited. The lock to the storage area was broken, and scrape marks show the barrel was dragged out. And in the third building there's evidence that a flammable liquid was poured in the center of the first floor."

"Whoever started the third fire knew a lot about how it would spread," the younger of the two men volunteered.

"Do you have someone in mind?" Brock asked.

The two men glanced at each other before the older one answered. "Let's say we will make that news public when we press criminal charges."

"Do you have the motive?" Brock asked.

The older man grinned at Mr. Everett. "You got a smart kid there. He figures if he knew the motive he'd have the suspect." Turning to Brock he asked, "Maybe you should be a detective when you grow up—Brock, was it? Thought about it?"

Brock flushed. "Yes sir," he admitted. "I've thought about it."

Over the next week things settled down to pretty much of a routine. Mr. Long steadily improved, but he still talked out of his head so much that he was no help to anyone.

The new house was beginning to take shape. Brock pedaled out twice, once to write his initials in the concrete foundation and once to collect wood scraps for one of Marilla's school projects. The trees in the area were pretty. Maybe it wouldn't be so bad being in a new neighborhood.

In his spare time, Brock went to the library and rummaged through old newspapers. He read about fires in apartments for the past six months.

In two cases apartment projects had been temporarily stopped by court injunctions several weeks before the buildings burned down. People living in the areas had objected to apartment buildings being so close to them. There had been some speculation that maybe someone set the fires to permanently stop the projects.

But Brock could find no record of protests or problems with the other four buildings.

He took an old note pad from school and made notes about the fires. He determined that they usually happened early in the week or toward the end of the week. He didn't know if this was an important clue or not.

The fires had occurred only in partially finished apartments. He wondered if that was because the projects were costing too much money to complete or because the firebug didn't want to endanger people's lives.

Brock told Gaby about his discoveries one afternoon as they bolted his train track onto the finished board. There was no way he could talk to her about his suspicions of her father, so he focused on Humphrey.

"I shouldn't have removed that medallion from the scene," he told Gaby. "I especially shouldn't have given it back to Humphrey. That was evidence."

"I saw you give it to him," Gaby reminded Brock. "I could testify to that."

Brock laughed hollowly. "We two aren't exactly disinterested parties. You're the owner's daughter and my dad is the foreman. A slick lawyer could make the jury think I hid the medallion in my pocket and just told you I found it there. They'd throw me in jail before they'd jail someone on my testimony."

"But his mother saw you give Humphrey the medallion!" Gaby reminded him.

"She's not disinterested, either! Do you really think she'd testify against her own son in court?"

"Then we need better proof," Gaby said. "We'll just have to get it."

"We need proof they can't ignore," Brock told her.

Gaby tossed the screwdriver back into the toolbox. "I feel so sorry for Humphrey, don't you?"

Brock nodded. "If he did start the fires, at least our proving it would get him some help."

"If?" Gaby echoed. "*If?* You mean you still have doubts? If not Humphrey, then who?"

Brock was not prepared to answer that. He hooked a tanker car and caboose to the engine. He signaled Gaby to plug in the electrical cord. His eyes followed the train as it slowly clattered around the track.

If only all the clues fit together as snugly as the cars of the train. And if only the solution didn't seem to involve Gaby's father.

But nothing could be worse than not knowing.

"There's only one thing to do," Brock told Gaby. "We are going to have to follow Humphrey. We have got to know for sure, one way or the other."

14

"Us? Follow Humphrey?" Gaby asked Brock.

The car barrier dropped into place on the train board and the flashing light signaled the approaching train. At least something was working right, Brock thought. He hoped their following Humphrey would work out as well.

"We might even catch him in the act," Brock said, feeling a little guilty about hoping Humphrey was a firebug. But at least that would prove Gaby's father was innocent. Of course, there were still the problems of the switched appliances and Mr. Long's accident and Mr. Gifford's wanting to call off the investigation...

But he had to take one step at a time, Brock told himself. He had to build the case carefully, just like the layers of landscape on the train board.

"What if that is what Mr. Long did?" Gaby interrupted his thoughts. "I mean, what if Mr. Long was hurt because he caught Humphrey, or whoever, in the act of setting a fire? Won't we be in danger if someone catches us?"

Danger? They might be, at that, Brock realized. "Maybe you'd better not come with me," he said.

"Don't be a nut!" Gaby retorted. "If you go, I go."

After school the next day, Brock and Gaby watched from behind the hall lockers until they saw Humphrey leave his last class. They followed him at a safe distance as he left campus. To their surprise, the Hump headed straight into the neighborhood fire station.

"Maybe he's going to confess," Brock offered hopefully.

It seemed like hours until Humphrey emerged from the station. Brock glanced at his watch. Only twenty minutes had gone by.

"Stick with him," Brock told Gaby. "I'm going inside to find out what he said. Just stay out of sight and you'll be all right. I'll wait for you at your house."

Brock walked past the gleaming white fire engines to a small door. Inside was the recreation room. Some of the men and women were playing checkers, reading, or watching TV.

"Hi," one of the men greeted Brock. "Can I help you?"

"I'd like to ask some questions," Brock told him.

"Sure," the man said. "You writing a school report?"

Brock blushed, wishing he'd thought of that as a cover. "Is that what the other boy wanted?" he asked.

The man shoved a coin into the soft-drink machine. "Can I get you something?"

When Brock shook his head no, the man punched the button marked *grape* and waited until the can dropped with a loud clunk into the trough. He pulled the tab and took a sip.

"Humphrey? Naw. He's one of our regulars," the man said at last.

"A regular?" Brock asked. "Isn't that a little— weird?"

The man shrugged. "Weird? Maybe, but if it is, then half of us in this room are a little weird. I hung around a fire station when I was a kid. I'd drive 'em crazy wanting to help shine the engine."

"Did you watch fires?" Brock asked him. "Take pictures, stuff like that?"

The man took another sip from the can as he studied Brock's face. Brock flushed.

"Look, you can't be too good a friend of Humphrey's or you'd have a pretty good idea about what makes him tick."

"I don't know him too well, but I guess you could say I'm as close to him as anybody."

The man clicked his tongue against his teeth. "Figures. He would have a hard time making friends. He's too eager."

"I'd like to know him better," Brock said honestly. "Maybe you could tell me about his visits?"

"Poor kid wants to be a fire fighter," the man said. "But he'll never make it with all that extra weight. He's half a boy overweight. The work is hard. There are weight limits."

Brock felt a rush of anger and confusion. "Why doesn't he do something about his weight, if he wants to be a fire fighter so much?"

"I don't know." The man motioned for Brock to sit. "Humphrey's father was a fire fighter, but Humphrey never knew him. The guy took too much smoke too many times and was finally transferred to the main office—away from the action, sort of. He became the official company photographer. You know, he took pictures of fires for the records."

He took a sip from his grape can. "Humphrey's

old man was a good photographer, too. He just didn't know what fear was. He got some of the scariest shots you can imagine—the kind that showed people what it was like to be inside a furnace, trying to fight your way out with an ax and a hose."

The man leaned back with a shrug. "He was inside a burning building one day when it collapsed on him. Humphrey was born three days after the funeral. I guess in a way Humphrey uses us as his fathers. Anyway, he started secretly hanging around here the minute he could toddle."

"Secretly?" Brock asked. "Why secretly?"

"His mother used to drag him away screaming and kickin'. She'd lost a husband to a fire. I guess she didn't want her only kid to be a fire fighter, too."

"Wow!" Brock said. "I had no idea!"

The man took the last sip from the can, then aimed and threw it into the trash container across the room.

A raucous buzz sounded above them, reverberating off the slick walls so that it seemed to come from every direction. Chairs scraped and feet shuffled past Brock so fast that he felt he was in the eye of a hurricane. The building shuddered as the heavy engines of the hook-and-ladder and pumper trucks turned over. With their sirens blaring a warning to pedestrians and drivers, the trucks rumbled away. In less than twenty seconds, Brock was completely alone.

He stood a moment, staring around him at the empty station. Then he left.

As he trudged toward Gaby's house, Brock remembered how Humphrey's mother had offered them all those fattening foods. Didn't she know that she could be responsible for her son being disqualified for the only job he really wanted?

Was it frustration that drove Humphrey to maybe even setting fires? For the first time Brock hoped that he and Gaby wouldn't find any evidence against Humphrey.

But he didn't want to find evidence against Mr. Gifford, either.

He saw Gaby running toward him and braced himself to hear the truth, whatever it was.

15

Gaby grabbed Brock's arm. She tugged him back toward her house as she spoke rapidly. "I followed Humphrey to the Melrose building today. That's one of Dad's apartment projects. Then he stopped off at the hardware store.

"Brock, he bought a two-and-a-half gallon gas can! He filled it at the service station and took it home. I figured he'd stay there until dark, at least, so I came back."

Brock shook his head sadly. "A gas can? Why? Unless he was planning to torch those apartments—?"

"Tonight?" Gaby asked fearfully. "We'd better tell somebody. At least my dad should know, don't you think?"

"Know what?" Brock said. "We don't have any real evidence."

They reached Gaby's front lawn. A car was

parked in front of the house. It was the car with the rental sticker on it. The screen door creaked open as they reached the porch.

"Talking ain't healthy!" the man growled as he shoved out onto the porch. "You just won't know trouble until you start talking. I can involve you up to your ears!"

Brock stared open-mouthed at the man. He could feel Gaby's grip on his arm tighten.

The man glared at Brock and Gaby as he shoved past them, got into his car, and drove away.

Mr. Gifford dabbed at his neck and forehead with a folded handkerchief. He seemed pale and shaken.

"Dad?" Gaby said, anxiety in her voice.

"Stay out of it," her father said sharply as he headed inside. "You kids just tend to your own business, you hear? And Gaby, you—you don't go anywhere unless you tell me, hear?"

Gaby seemed stunned by his words.

Brock patted her hand. "I've seen that creep somewhere before. And I'm positive he had a gun. There was a definite bulge on one side of his coat. What business could he have with your dad?"

"None!" Gaby argued. "Dad wouldn't have any business with someone like that!"

Brock snapped his fingers. "Wait a minute! Those pictures of Hump's. I think that guy was in some of them. I can't be sure, of course. They were blurred. Maybe if Humphrey could enlarge them I could tell."

"That will have to wait," Gaby reminded him. "We have to watch Humphrey. We have to keep him from doing anything awful."

"What about your dad? He'll never let you out of the house, especially so late at night."

Gaby shrugged. "He was upset by that terrible man, that's all. I'll get out of the house somehow. Maybe if we can solve this fire thing, he'll feel a lot better and start acting more like himself."

Brock arranged to meet Gaby around midnight. He decided to hurry home and eat with his folks so they wouldn't suspect anything, then maybe go to Humphrey's. Maybe, just maybe, he could stop him.

Brock shifted uneasily at supper. His father was giving them a report on the progress of the house, and right now the new house was the least of Brock's concerns.

"The painter got mad and sprayed our kitchen cabinets black," Sam Everett said. "Of course, I won't pay him a cent, but I'll still have to pay someone else to strip and redo them."

"As your resident lawyer," Gwen Everett said, "I can assure you it'd do little good to sue. The time and money we'd have to spend would far outweigh what we could get."

"I know," Sam Everett said grimly. "All I can do is see that the guy doesn't get work with anyone I know. I can't believe so many things have gone wrong."

Gwen Everett moaned. "I just hope we've seen the worst of it. But when I was out there this afternoon I saw that our plumber was the football quarterback when I was in high school—I hope he's better at putting in pipes than he was at playing football."

"At least one good thing happened today," Mr. Everett said. "Tom Long was released from the hospital."

Brock snapped to attention. "Did he say anything about what happened?"

"He told the investigators he heard something in one of the apartments during his regular rounds. He went in to investigate, and someone hit him. He's sure that's what happened, and he's sure the fire hadn't started yet."

Brock gasped. "But that means someone left him to die. That's attempted murder!"

His food seemed to stick in his throat. No matter which way he turned, the facts were getting uglier. But who was involved? Humphrey or Mr. Gifford?

"I need to do some research," Brock said after supper. He knew his parents would think he was at the library.

He pedaled over to Humphrey's.

Humphrey was in his front yard, pushing a droning lawn mower. Perspiration pasted his T-shirt to him. Sweat beads clung to his lashes and brows.

He grinned at Brock, who settled his bike against a tree and slid onto the porch step to watch.

The mower sputtered to a stop, and Humphrey abandoned it to plop onto the step beside Brock.

"Out of gas," he told Brock. "I'll have to let it cool down before I can gas it up again."

Brock nodded, his eyes falling on the new gas can that sat near the driveway. Could Humphrey have bought the can for the mower?

"How about a nice cool malted milk while you're resting?" Humphrey's mother called through the screen door.

Brock felt anger welling up inside him. "For crying out loud, Humphrey. Tell her you just want water, will you?"

"Would you like me better?" Humphrey asked, a light whine in his voice.

"For Pete's sake," Brock said. "Drink what you want."

Humphrey called back over his shoulder, "Just water, please." He looked back at Brock as if waiting for approval.

Brock obliged him. "You did good, Hump."

Brock stared at his feet, trying to get up the nerve to ask Humphrey what he'd come here to ask. "Do you know anything about the apartment fires?" he asked at last. "Can you tell me anything at all?"

Humphrey shook his head. "I might. But I don't want to hurt her. You understand?"

Brock's skin prickled. He knew he was close to hearing the truth now. Humphrey had all but said he was keeping quiet so he wouldn't hurt his mother.

"You know we—they—will find the truth eventually, Hump."

"It's hard being one kid with a single parent," Hump said. "I don't want to hurt her."

"Think about it, Hump," Brock said, walking toward his bike. "We can all help. Honest."

He pushed off on his bike, glancing back toward Humphrey.

He was leaning over the lawn mower, filling it again.

Brock pedaled toward home. It was getting dark. He felt as though his insides were going to explode. He really wanted to tell his folks what he and Gaby were going to do tonight. But what could he say? He didn't have any real evidence. It would be better to wait until he had proof.

His parents were still talking about the house and paid little attention to his nervousness. He made an excuse and went to his room early.

Brock sat in the dark, watching the luminous hands of his watch move ever so slowly toward midnight. At a quarter of twelve he stood with his ear to his door, listening to see if there were signs of life in the house.

All was quiet. He tiptoed down the hall. The door to Marilla's room eased shut as he passed it.

16

When Gaby and Brock reached the Melrose apartment project, they found that a light was burning in the security guard's shack. But the rest of the project was lighted only by moonlight that filtered through a low cloud cover.

"What if we guessed wrong?" Gaby whispered. "What if while we are watching this building Humphrey torches one across town instead? What if I misunderstood his visit here today?"

Brock had serious doubts, too. Gaby could be right. They could be at the wrong place, or they could have come on the wrong night. And even if Humphrey was going to set fire to this project, what could they do to stop him? In his rush to find evidence Brock hadn't thought that far ahead.

"Look!" Gaby whispered, pointing. "Isn't that someone in the shadows?"

Brock stared into the darkness, waiting until his eyes had adjusted. Then he saw the dark figure, too. A bulky form moved cautiously through one of the main units.

"It's Humphrey," Brock said. He felt a chill run through his whole body.

The moonlight played off something shiny.

"He's got the gas can," Brock whispered. "We'd better hurry."

They scrambled across the scattered boards and debris toward a door where they saw Humphrey disappear. Brock paused at the door.

"Maybe you'd better stay out here," he whispered.

But Gaby shook her head stubbornly. "I didn't come this far to wait outside."

Brock slowly opened the door. It was so quiet he could hear himself breathing. His nose filled with the odors of sawdust and paint, perfect materials for a fire.

He and Gaby looked around the dark room.

"You bring the flashlight?" Brock whispered.

His answer was the cool metal cylinder shoved into his hand. He flicked it on, moving the light slowly around the room. The light caught a slight movement in the corner. Brock brought the flashlight up to shine directly on Humphrey's pale and sweating face.

"Brock! Gaby!" Humphrey cried.

"It's all over, Humphrey," Brock said. "You can't do this. We won't let you."

"But you don't understand. I've just got to!" Humphrey argued.

"No you don't! We can help you. We won't let you torch these apartments," Brock continued. "Give me the gas can."

"The what?" Humphrey yelled. "Torch the apartments! Are you crazy? Why would I want to do that?"

"Why else are you here?" Brock demanded.

Humphrey lifted his camera into the flashlight's beam. "I am here to get evidence. If I can actually take a picture of the firebug setting the fire, that will be the best evidence there is. You mean you thought—"

"Well, why wouldn't we?" Brock said. "You are absolutely nuts over fires. And you told me you didn't want to hurt your mother with the truth."

"My mother!" Humphrey shrieked. "I wasn't talking about my mother!"

"Shhh!" Gaby interrupted. "Turn off the light. Someone's coming."

The three of them scrambled into a closet and pulled the door almost shut behind them. They huddled together, trying to get a peek through the crack they'd left.

The outside door opened. A stream of light cut through the darkness. Someone else was looking around the room.

"The watchman?" Gaby whispered.

"I don't think so, but I can't see his face," Brock whispered back.

The dark figure set the light on a nail keg, then moved around in front of it to bend over a barrel. His face was suddenly caught in the light. It was the man with the rental car who'd been arguing with Mr. Gifford.

Brock was so startled that he jerked backward, knocking Humphrey's camera against the closet wall with a dull thud.

The three of them held their breath as the man paused, looking in their direction. His mouth jerked into a quick smile as he continued to work in the light.

"Did he see us?" Gaby asked.

"I don't think so," Brock said. "Look."

The man had a gasoline can. He sloshed liquid

110

against the walls. He moved in their direction, and the three of them shrank from the crack.

The closet door suddenly pushed closed with a slam, shutting out the little light they'd had. There was a scraping noise, then something thudded against the door.

There was no need to keep quiet now, Brock realized. The man had known they were there all the time. He'd pushed something against the door. It held fast.

Brock slammed his shoulder against the door, but it didn't budge.

There was an explosive poof outside the closet, followed by cracking, popping sounds.

"He's torched the room!" Brock yelled. "We're trapped!"

17

"I can't budge it!" Brock screamed. "Push! Hurry!"

Frantically the three of them shoved against the door. Smoke seeped under the door crack. They gagged from its denseness.

"Cover your faces!" Humphrey yelled. "Three whiffs of this stuff and you'll pass out!"

He ripped the shirt from his back and tore it into strips. He, Gaby, and Brock tied the strips over their noses. "Spit on them!" Humphrey said. "Moisten the strips to keep out the smoke." He crammed the rest of his shirt into the crack under the door.

"Drop to the floor," he ordered. "Smoke rises."

Obediently Brock and Gaby dropped to their knees.

The door was fiercely hot now. Brock touched the handle and cried out in pain from the searing heat. "Its no use!" he screamed. "We can't just wait here for the fire to reach us!"

His eyes burned. He could feel the oxygen being consumed by the intense fire just outside the door. He clutched Gaby's hand tightly. He felt her squeeze back. All the things he'd said and thought about Humphrey flashed back to him and he felt a tightening in his throat.

"Humphrey," he said, "I—I'm sorry."

Humphrey was standing on a cinder block, poking at the ceiling. "Never mind that now," he said. "Help me. If I can find the trapdoor, maybe we can get into the next apartment. Hurry."

In his panic Brock had forgotten about the trapdoors that were sometimes in closets. Repairmen used them to get into attics.

He boosted Gaby up. She searched frantically with her fingers and shouted, "It's here!"

"Push it open and climb up through it!" Brock said. "The attics are all joined together—I remember Dad told me. We can crawl through this attic and down into the closet in the next apartment."

But Gaby scrambled down. "No. It'll take us both to boost Humphrey."

Smoke continued to seep into the closet.

"No, Gaby!" Humphrey shouted. "You go first!"

"Don't argue!" she screamed. "Now!"

Brock and Gaby struggled under Humphrey's weight but finally got him to where he could help himself through the hole. Brock lifted Gaby up next.

Then he reached up and felt four hands grab him. "Hurry!" he shouted. "The smoke is getting fierce."

Brock's shoulders ached as he finally pulled himself into the attic. "This way," he said.

He felt along the attic floor until his fingers touched another cover. Shoving it to the side, he dropped through the hole and then yelled for Gaby to drop down. Humphrey tumbled through last.

They were in another closet. Smoke wafted through cracks. Already the heat in this apartment was bad. Suddenly one of the closet walls exploded into flames as the fire broke through.

Gaby screamed.

"Grab hands!" Brock shouted. He shoved open the closet door and led them out of the closet, the fire fighter's words echoing in his brain. "It was like being inside a furnace." Now he knew what that was like. Only he and Gaby and Humphrey were fighting their way out bare-handed.

They dashed to the front door of the apartment. Brock yelled in pain as he forced himself to grab the handle and pull the door open. The three of them stumbled outside.

Humphrey sank to the ground, coughing and choking. Brock and Gaby pulled at him, urging him to hurry. They had to get farther away from the burning building.

Panting and wheezing from the smoke inhalation, Humphrey obediently pulled himself to his feet just as the apartment window shattered with explosive force behind them.

Brock cried out as splinters of glass pricked at his skin. Half stumbling, he headed toward the lighted security shack. Brock pushed through the door.

"Fire!" he yelled, still trying to catch his breath. "Call the fire department. And the police—hurry!"

The guard, who'd been obviously relaxed with his feet on his desk, whirled to face Brock and the orange glow behind him.

The man dove for the phone, dialed the fire department, then barked the address into the receiver. When the guard had dialed the police, Brock grabbed the phone.

"Tall guy," he said. "Arsonist. Attempted murder. Dark hair. Greenish eyes, I think. Car from Reynolds Rental Agency. I don't know his name—"

"It's Stafford," a voice behind Brock said. "Marvin Stafford."

"You can tell them we already have him," Mr. Gifford said. He motioned toward the door as Sam Everett pushed the man in the gray suit into the shack.

Numbly Brock relayed the information to the police. "But how did you get here so fast?" he asked his father. "How did you know?"

Mr. Everett rushed over to hug his son. "Marilla saw you leave and told me," he said, smiling slightly. "Marched right in, woke us up, and demanded the right to go out at night, too."

Brock laughed. "Remind me to hug that little monkey," he said.

Gaby came in with Humphrey. "Daddy!" she said.

Mr. Gifford hugged his daughter. "When Sam called about Brock being missing and I couldn't find you, we sort of put that together and figured you two were up to something crazy like this. I'd already warned the arson investigators about Stafford. They were looking for him, too."

"When we saw your bikes and Stafford's car here, we knew we had the right place," Mr. Everett added. "I guess the investigators started checking at the other end of town."

116

"Yeah," Mr. Gifford said, planting a kiss on Gaby and shaking Humphrey's hand. "I just wish we'd found you on the first try instead of the second—you had a narrow escape."

Brock shuddered, thinking what might have happened. "Second try?"

"When Garwood figured out what Stafford was up to, he confronted him with it. Stafford threatened to torch everything Garwood owned. And he threatened if Garwood told on him, he'd swear that Garwood was in on the arson with him. Which he wasn't, of course," Mr. Everett added. "So we started checking Gifford's buildings and you were at the second one we checked."

The sirens were approaching from a distance. Or were those bells suddenly going off in his head? Brock wondered. Something finally dawned on him. It had been *Gaby* that Humphrey didn't want to hurt, not his own mother. Somehow Humphrey must have been putting the puzzle together, too, and must have come up with Mr. Gifford as the answer. Of course, the Hump had the advantage of knowing that he was innocent.

Brock could hear the sounds of pumpers outside as they forced water onto the blaze. "I just couldn't

117

believe that you were involved, Mr. Gifford," Brock said.

"I'm glad to hear that!" Garwood Gifford replied. "I can assure you, I'm not!"

While the fire fighters battled the blaze, Mr. Gifford explained what had happened.

"I got my finances just too spread out and building costs kept rising. I was in trouble. I tried to sell out at cost, but nobody would buy. I couldn't blame them. They couldn't make any profit on the projects, either. Then this guy came to me. He offered to buy me out, but said I had to keep quiet about it—pretend I was still the owner." He laughed hollowly. "He said it was better if folks still thought they were dealing with a local. I was so glad to be bailed out I didn't stop to think why he wanted the projects. Of course I sold at a loss. But that gave me enough to hold on to two of the projects and keep them going."

Mr. Gifford continued. "Out of the original six projects, I own only the one at Morgan and Pierce and whatever is left of this one. The others are owned by Stafford, or rather by his syndicate."

The police and arson officers soon arrived to arrest Marvin Stafford. "This is gonna clear up about eighteen unsolved fires," the older officer said. "Thanks for your cooperation, Mr. Gifford.

"The syndicate spreads across five states," the officer continued. "Quite a profit-making organization, too. Might not have caught on to their location if someone hadn't jimmied one of those old appliances open from one of the fire sites. As soon as we traced them to another state, we started putting two and two together."

Brock felt his chest swell with pride. He'd helped catch the arsonist, after all.

"Until we found out that the appliances were old," Mr. Gifford said, "I just couldn't get it into my head that the fires weren't accidents. Stafford convinced me that nobody would have all the appliances delivered and then torch a place. There wouldn't be any profit in that."

"We think now the appliance business was just a smoke screen Stafford threw up. The insurance return on the appliances wouldn't be so great. But the early delivery threw us off the track for a while. The usual arson pattern is to stop all deliveries before torching a place," the older arson investigator said.

"The rise in the cost of appliances hasn't been very great," said the younger officer. "There wouldn't be much profit in getting replacement insurance on them. But the project itself, now that's another tale!"

Brock scratched his head. "How could they make so much money on the project?

The younger man's face brightened, obviously pleased that he had a ready answer. "It takes a year or more to build a project like this. This area has been behind the rest of the country for a long time in building costs. But now it's moving faster than the rest of the country—trying to catch up, you might say. It's increased about ten per cent a month this year. The replacement insurance must reflect the future inflated building cost."

"Wow!" Brock said. "I get it! That's a hundred and twenty percent increase in a year. But wouldn't all the insurance money be spent in rebuilding?"

The older man interrupted his assistant. "The syndicate has no intention of rebuilding. They can stall a while, collect their money, pretend to be regrouping, then vanish. They've pulled this in five states so far and probably planned to try it in the other forty-five states, too."

"The night Mr. Long was hurt I had to face the possibility that these fires were no accidents," Mr. Gifford said, hugging Gaby to him. "I began to see why Stafford made me replace the guards on the places his syndicate owned. But I had refused to replace Mr. Long, poor man.

"I went to the arson investigators with what I had. We worked together. But I should have told you kids. You might have been killed! After I confronted Stafford, he must have found out I was working with the police. I had no idea he'd try to get even like this!"

The fire captain stuck his head inside. "Fire's out," he said. "The unit where the fire started is totaled. But the rest are okay."

"Gee, I feel so stupid," Humphrey said. "I should've told my friends at the firehouse what I was doing. But I wanted to help Gaby. I wanted to gather evidence about the firebug. I didn't want her dad to be in trouble. I know what it's like to be only half a family."

"But, Humphrey," Gaby asked, "how did you know this building was the next one Stafford would torch?"

Humphrey grinned. "You two aren't the only ones who can snoop. I saw that guy too many times in my pictures. He was just too close to the fires not to be involved some way. I followed him. He sat out in his car, staring at this project a long time. And I could see he had some blueprints spread out over his steering wheel."

The fire was almost out. The paramedics checked Gaby and Humphrey and treated Brock's burned hands and face.

"You know what?" Humphrey said, still clutching his camera tightly. "I forgot to take pictures."

Later, as Brock drove away with his father, he looked back toward the blackened skeleton of the unit where he, Humphrey, and Gaby had been trapped. He shuddered, thinking of those terrifying moments in the closet. Some detective he'd turned out to be!

He wondered if Humphrey could ever forgive him for suspecting him. Could Gaby forgive him for suspecting her father? Could he forgive himself?

18

Brock, Humphrey, and Gaby sat on the floor of the Everett's living room weeks later, wrapping cups and vases for the big move. Brock's burns had healed, but he was still troubled by what had happened.

"I still feel awful about thinking you started those fires, Humphrey," he admitted.

Humphrey carefully placed a wrapped cup into the straw-filled barrel. "You feel bad! I guess a lot of that I brought on myself by acting suspicious on purpose. I liked the attention. Besides, all my evidence was pointing to Mr. Gifford, so I felt pretty awful, too. I didn't know he'd sold his buildings. I thought he'd hired Stafford to do the torching."

Brock still remembered how Humphrey hadn't wanted to say anything that might hurt Gaby. He was a good friend, after all.

Gaby nodded sympathetically. "I wasn't all that

123

nice about your father, Brock. After all, I accused him of being careless. If only Daddy had let us know he didn't own those apartments, that he'd secretly sold out in order to keep his last two without going bankrupt.''

She reached to wrap a candy bowl. There were still three pieces inside. "Chocolate?" she offered.

"Not for me!" Humphrey said. "That fire sure convinced me I need to get in shape. But I intend to be by the time I'm out of high school—I guarantee.''

Brock grinned. "Way to go, Hump.''

As the last of the moving vans pulled away, Mrs. Everett came in. "Come on, everybody. Let's head for the new house and do all of this in reverse.''

Groaning, they piled into the car. Soon they pulled to a stop in front of the new rambling brick ranch.

Marilla, who'd gone over earlier with Mr. Everett, skipped out to greet them. "Mommy!" she shouted. "You didn't tell me we'd have an indoor swimming pool! Can I put on my bathing suit?''

The four of them paused, staring in puzzlement at one another, then broke into a full run.

"Sam?" Mrs. Everett wailed as she pushed through the front door. "Sam!''

Their feet sloshed through nearly an inch of water that covered the sunken living-room floor. Sam Everett stood in the living room, feet apart, hands on his hips and eyes on the ceiling. Brock's eyes followed his gaze. The plaster board above them bulged with water that streamed through a crack.

"Unsealed pipe, I suppose. Didn't show up until we turned on the water," Sam Everett suggested.

Marilla made slapping noises as she stomped through the water in her bare feet.

"Oh, blast that quarterback!" Mrs. Everett shrieked. "I knew he'd be a lousy plumber!"

"Just think of this as the latest thing in fire prevention," Humphrey said. "You have your own water supply ready for any emergency."

Brock knew they'd have to rip a hole in the ceiling and seal the pipe. Then they'd have to replaster and patch and bail water. But he couldn't help it—he broke into a fit of laughter all the same.

"But it's home!" he yelled. "Welcome home, everybody!"

Instinctively he reached to hug Gaby to him, enjoying the sound of her laughter. He led her to the patio, away from the others.

"You said once you weren't ready to be more

than a friend," he reminded her. "Now that our lives are back in order, do you think you're ready to go steady with a freckle-faced redhead who stumbles over his own feet?" he asked.

Gaby tweaked his nose playfully. "You call yourself a super snoop, Brock Everett. But you don't see right before your nose!"

Brock lifted an eyebrow in puzzlement.

Gaby grinned. "We've been 'steady' all along!"

About the Author

When Mary Blount Christian was in the fifth grade, her teacher had her stand up in front of the class every day after lunch and tell a continuing suspense story involving other children in the room. The young storyteller quickly learned that her audience stayed interested if the tale had lots of action.

Mrs. Christian's journalism studies at the University of Houston and her work as a free-lance newspaper reporter sharpened her ability to grab and hold readers' attention. Over the years she has come to care more for the "why" of a news story than for the plain facts, and as a result she has become devoted to the writing of fiction.

Mary Blount Christian likes to write stories that are humorous or mysterious, and she's especially delighted when she can combine both qualities in her work. When she isn't writing, she's talking about writing with children or teaching writing in the classroom, on television, or via a correspondence school.